U0088389

Useful English
Vocabulary

無敵 英語
單字王

國家圖書館出版品預行編目資料

無敵英語單字王 / 張瑜凌編著

-- 初版. -- 新北市：雅典文化, 民111.06

面；　公分. -- (行動學習；19)

ISBN 978-626-95952-2-8(平裝)

1. CST: 英語　2. CST: 詞彙

805.12　　　　　　　　　　　111006589

行動學習系列　19

無敵英語單字王

編　　著／張瑜凌
責任編輯／張文娟
內文排版／鄭孝儀
封面設計／林鈺恆

掃描填回函
好書隨時抽

法律顧問：方圓法律事務所／涂成樞律師

總經銷：永續圖書有限公司
永續圖書線上購物網
www.foreverbooks.com.tw

出版日／2022年06月

雅典文化

出版社　22103　新北市汐止區大同路三段194號9樓之1
　　　　　TEL　(02) 8647-3663
　　　　　FAX　(02) 8647-3660

Phonics 自然發音規則對照表

看得懂英文字卻不會念？還是看不懂也不會念？沒關係，跟著此自然發音規則對照表，看字讀音、聽音拼字，另附中文輔助，你就能念出7成左右常用的英文字喔！

自然發音規則，主要分為子音、母音、結合子音與結合母音這四大組。

◎第1組—子音規則

【b】貝 -bag 袋子	【c】克 -car 車子	【d】的 -door 門
【f】夫 -fat 肥胖的	【g】個 -gift 禮物	【h】賀 -house 房子
【j】這 -joke 笑話	【k】克 -key 鑰匙	【l】樂 -light 燈光
【m】麼 -man 男人 (母音前)	【m】嗯 -ham 火腿 (母音後，閉嘴)	【n】呢 -nice 好的 (母音前，張嘴)
【n】嗯 -can 可以 (母音後)	【p】配 -park 公園	【qu】擴- quiet 安靜
【r】若 -red 紅色	【s】思 -start 開始	【t】特 -test 測驗
【v】富 -voice 聲音	【w】握 -water 水	【x】克思 -x-ray x光
【y】意 -yes 是的	【z】日 -zoo 動物園	

◎第2組─母音規則

短母音		
【a】欸(嘴大) -ask 詢問	【e】欸(嘴小) -egg 蛋	【i】意 -inside 裡面
【o】啊 -hot 熱的	【u】餓 -up 向上	
長母音		
【a】欸意 -aid 幫助	【e】意 -eat 吃	【i】愛 -lion 獅子
【o】歐 -old 老的	【u】物 -you 你	

◎第3組—結合子音規則

【ch】 去 -chair 椅子	【sh】 噓 -share 分享	【gh】 個 -ghost 鬼
【ph】 夫 -phone 電話	【wh】 或 -what 什麼	【rh】 若 -rhino 犀牛
【th】 思 -thin 瘦的 (伸出舌頭，無聲)	【th】 日 -that 那個 (伸出舌頭，有聲)	【bl】 貝樂 -black 黑的
【cl】 克樂 -class 班級	【fl】 夫樂 -flower 花朵	【gl】 個樂 -glass 玻璃
【pl】 配樂 -play 玩耍	【sl】 思樂 -slow 慢的	【br】 貝兒 -break 打破
【cr】 擴兒 -cross 橫越	【dr】 桌兒 -dream 夢	【fr】 佛兒 -free 自由的
【gr】 過兒 -great 優秀的	【pr】 配兒 -pray 祈禱	【tr】 綽兒 -train 火車
【wr】 若 -write 寫字	【kn】 呢 -know 知道	【mb】 嗯(閉嘴) -comb 梳子
【ng】 嗯(張嘴) -sing 唱歌	【tch】 去 -catch 捉住	【sk】 思個 -skin 皮膚
【sm】 思麼 -smart 聰明	【sn】 思呢 -snow 雪	【st】 思的 -stop 停止
【sp】 思貝 -speak 說話	【sw】 思握 -sweater 毛衣	

◎第4組—結合母音規則

【ai】欸意	【ay】欸意	【aw】歐
-rain	-way	-saw
雨水	方式	鋸子
【au】歐	【ea】意	【ee】意
-sauce	-seat	-see
醬汁	座位	看見
【ei】欸意	【ey】欸意	【ew】物
-eight	-they	-new
八	他們	新的
【ie】意	【oa】歐	【oi】喔意
-piece	-boat	-oil
一片	船	油
【oo】物	【ou】澳	【ow】歐
-food	-outside	-grow
食物	外面	成長
【oy】喔意	【ue】物	【ui】物
-boy	-glue	-fruit
男孩	膠水	水果
【a_e】欸意	【e_e】意	【i_e】愛
-game	-delete	-side
遊戲	刪除	邊、面
【o_e】歐	【u_e】物	【ci】思
-hope	-use	-circle
希望	使用	圓圈
【ce】思	【cy】思	【gi】句
-center	-cycle	-giant
中心	循環	巨人
【ge】句	【gy】句	【ar】啊兒
-gentle	-gym	-far
溫和的	體育館	遠的
【er】兒	【ir】兒	【or】歐兒
-enter	-bird	-order
輸入	小鳥	順序
【ur】兒	【igh】愛	【ind】愛嗯的
-burn	-high	-find
燃燒	高的	找到

※ 小試身手：

現在你可以運用上述自然發音的規則，試念以下這些句子：

★ Anything wrong?

★ It's time for bed.

★ Let's go for a ride.

★ May I use the phone?

★ Nice to meet you.

★ That sounds good.

★ I feel thirsty.

★ Turn off the light, please.

★ May I leave now?

★ Here you are.

● 【前言】

史上超強，實用英文單字字庫！！

想要學好英文，到底要背哪些單字才夠呢？

每次要開口說英文時，老是覺得自己的單字背得不夠多嗎？

若是曾經在面對要說英文的場合，出現上述這種總是詞窮的窘境，就表示你需要再加強英文單字的背誦了！至於哪些單字是你的首選必背名單，本書「無敵英語1500單字」不但匯集了超過1500個單字，也是大學以上程度所需的字彙，幫助您加強英文單字的使用實力。

「無敵英語1500單字」所匯集的字彙均著重在生活化的用法，不論是在生活或工作場合中都適用，範圍囊括閒談、搭訕、問候等，建議可以先從比較簡單的句子開始記憶，並隨書附 MP3 伴讀光碟，由外師隨文導讀錄音，建議您可以隨外師的音調、速度一同大聲朗讀，以加強您的英文實力。此外，本書還匯集了「常見縮寫」單元，幫助您記憶一些常見的縮寫用法。

單字不是會背就好，還必須應用在會話中。本書將單字套用在會話中,並衍生出相關的用法,幫助您在會話對談中能夠順利應用。同時還有類似單字的舉例以及衍生單字,讓您只要花一半的時間,就能同時記住單字和英語會話。

track 002

•I

pron. 我（第一人稱單數）

例 句

例 I usually take a walk after supper.
我通常在晚飯後散步。

例 I shouldn't have gone to see a movie last week.
我上星期不應該去看電影。

you

prop. 你、你們（第二人稱單、複數）

例 句

例 You have no idea, do you?
你完全不知道，對吧？

例 You know what?
你知道嗎？

he

pron. 他（第三人稱男性單數）

例 句

例 He had a terrible hangover after the party.
他在派對之後有嚴重的宿醉。

例 He is my younger brother. track 003
他是我的弟弟。

she

pron. 她（第三人稱女性單數）

例 句

例 She handed him a napkin.
她遞給了他一條餐巾。

例 She gave me some advice.
她給了我一些建議。

we

pron. 我們（第一人稱複數）

例 句

例 We are not friends anymore.
我們絕交了！

例 We should pick her up at her place.
我們應該去她家接她。

they

pron. 他們（第三人稱複數）

例 句

例 They are my parents.
他們是我的父母。

例 They always laugh at me.
他們總是嘲笑我。

track 003

it

pron.

這、那、它（指已提及的人、事、物，包含人、嬰兒、動物，與性別無關）、泛指時間、氣候、距離等無人稱動詞的主詞、受格

相關 **its** *pron.* 它的

例 句

例 "Are you David Jones?" "Yes, it's me."

「你是大衛・瓊斯嗎？」「是的，我就是！」

例 It's early yet.

時間還得很呢！

例 It's none of your business.

不關你的事！

例 "Is this a dog?" "Yes, it is."

「這是一隻狗嗎？」「是啊，它是！」

例 It rains.

下雨了！

track 004

this

pron. adj. 這個(人、事、物)

反義 **that** *adj. pron.* 那個

例 句

例 This is my wife Tracy.

這是我的太太崔西。

例 Who told you this?

這事是誰告訴你的？

例 Why are you doing this?

你為什麼要這麼做？

例 I don't like this room.

我不喜歡這間房間。

these

pron. adj. 這些（this 的複數）

例 句

例 These are my balls.

這些是我的球。

例 These books are a bit difficult for David.

這些書對大衛來說有一點太難。

例 These days, we hardly speak to each other.

我們現在很少說話了！

that

pron. adj. 那、那個(人、事、物)

例 句

例 That's impossible.

不可能的！

例 Look at that.

瞧瞧那個！

例 Who told you that story?

誰告訴你那個故事的？

track 004

those

pron. adj. 那些（that 的複數）

例 句

例 Listen, those houses are huge.

聽我說，那些房子很大。

例 Those big suitcases won't fit in the trunk.

那些行李不適合放在行李廂裡。

am

v. 是（用於第一人稱單數現在式）

例 句

例 I am supposed to go on a diet.

track 005

我應該要節食。

例 I am lost.

我迷路了。

相關單字

☑ was 是（用於第一、第三人稱單數 am/is 的過去式）

☞ I was a singer.

我以前是歌手！

☞ He was there.

他人就在那裡。

☞ It was a terrible accident.

真是可怕的意外。

is

v. 是(用於第三人稱單數現在式)

例 句

例 He is a student at the University of California.

他是加州大學的學生。

例 She is too little to ride a bicycle.

她年紀太小了，不能騎自行車。

例 David is always friendly.

大衛總是友善。

are

v. 是（用於第一人稱複數、第二人稱單、複數現在式，第三人稱複數現在式）

例 句

例 We are going to a party tomorrow.

明天我們要去參加一個派對。

例 You are a genius.

你真是聰明！

相關單字

☑ were 是（用於第一、第二人稱、第三人稱複數過去式）

☞ We were happy.

我們以前很快樂！

☞ They were my students.

他們以前是我的學生。

044

track 005

me

pron. 把我、對我（I 的受格）

例 句

例 The noise woke me up in the middle of the night.

在半夜我被噪音吵醒！

例 "Who did this to her?" "It's me."

「是誰對她做這件事的？」「是我！」

track 006

us

pron. 對我們（we 的受格）

例 句

例 It's difficult for us.

這對我們來說是困難的事。

例 Just tell us your idea.

只要告訴我們你的想法。

him

pron. 對他（he 的受格）

例 句

例 I can't see why you don't like him.

我不明白你為什麼不喜歡他。

例 The doctor advised him to have a rest.

醫生勸告他要休息。

her

pron. 對她（she 的受格）

例 句

例 I asked her to marry me.
我向她求婚。

例 Please ask her to call me back.
請她回我電話！

them

pron. 他們、它們（they 的受格）

例 句

例 Will you wrap them up?
能請你把它們包裝起來嗎？

例 I write to them once a month.
我每個月寫一次信給他們。

day

n. 日子、白天

例 句

例 There are seven days in a week.
一星期有七天。

例 Call me in the evening as I'm usually out during the day.
請在晚上打電話給我，因為我白天不在家。

例 He worked day and night.
他日以繼夜地工作。

衍生片語

☑ day and night　日日夜夜
☑ day after day　日復一日地
☑ every day　每天

 track 007

today

n.　今天
adv.　在今天

反義　yesterday *n. adv.* 昨天

例句

例 Today is David's birthday!
今天是大衛的生日！

例 Today is even hotter than yesterday!
今天甚至比昨天更熱。

例 We could go today or tomorrow.
我們可以今天或明天去。

nowadays

adv.　現今、時下

例句

例 Nowadays, people are lazy.
現在的人比較懶惰。

例 Nowadays, I bake my own bread rather than buy it.
現在我寧願自己烤麵包而不願用買的。

tomorrow

n.	明天、未來
adv.	在明天

例 句

例 Tomorrow is Sunday.

明天是星期天。

例 We are going to a party tomorrow.

明天我們要去參加一個派對。

例 He said he'll call tomorrow after work.

他說明天下班後他會來電。

衍生單字

☑ the day after tomorrow 後天

yesterday

n.	昨天、最近、近來
adv.	在昨天、近來

例 句

例 We had no classes yesterday.

昨天我們沒有課。

例 We got back from our vacation yesterday.

我們昨天才休假回來！

衍生單字

☑ the day before yesterday 前天

track 008

tonight

n. 今夜、今晚

adv. 在今晚

例 句

例 Tonight will be my first opportunity to meet her.

今天晚上是我第一次能見到她的機會。

例 Are you doing anything tonight?

你今天晚上有事嗎？

• morning

n. 早上、上午

例 句

例 Good morning, Jack.

傑克，早安！

例 I'll see you on Sunday morning.

星期天早上再見囉！

• afternoon

n. 下午、午後

例 句

例 She usually sleeps in the afternoon.

她通常會在下午睡覺。

例 Good afternoon.

午安!

evening

n. 傍晚

例 句

例 Good evening.

晚安!(晚上剛見面時的招呼語)

例 We always go to the movies on Friday evenings.

我們通常會在週五晚上去看電影!

例 I'll do my homework in the evening.

我將在晚上做我的作業。

night

n. 夜晚

例 句

例 Good night.

晚安再見!(晚上道別時的用語)

例 I'll be in Seattle on Tuesday night.

我週二晚上會到西雅圖。

例 It often gets cold here at night.

這裡晚上通常會冷。

track 009

深入分析

1. evening 通常是指在 afternoon 和 night 之間的時間，所以晚上見面通常會說"Good evening"，表示「祝你晚上好」的意思。

2. night 則多半指夜晚，所以晚上的道別要說；"Good night"，有祝你好眠的意味。

vacation

n. 假期、休假

例 句

例 They will spend their vacation abroad.
他們將到國外度假。

例 I'll have a vacation for six weeks.
我將有六個星期的假期。

深入分析

1. holiday 在英國指節日、紀念日、假日，也指學校、機關的假期。

2. vacation 在美國泛指一般假期，在英國專指學校、機關或法院休假日。

annual

adj. 每年的、年度的
n. 年刊、年鑒

例 句

例 David's annual income is $30,000.
大衛的年收入是三萬元。

daily

adj. 每日的、日常的
adv. 每日
n. 日刊

例 句

例 Exercise is part of my daily routine.
運動是我每日生活作息的一部份。

例 Take the pills twice daily.
這個藥丸每天要吃兩次。

weekly

adj. 每週的、一週一次的
adv. 一週一次地
n. 週報、週刊

例 句

例 At yesterday's weekly staff meeting the following points were discussed.
在昨天的全體人員每週例會上討論了如下幾點。

例 The New Scientist is published weekly.
《新科學家》每週出版一次。

 track 010

例 Many weeklies are full of stories about the new movie star.
許多週刊都刊登了關於這位電影新明星的各種故事。

monthly

adj.	每月的、每月一次的
adv.	每月地
n.	月刊

例 句

If you ride the bus a lot, you should buy a monthly ticket.

如果你經常搭公車，就應該要買月票。

We're paid monthly.

我們每個月支薪。

quarterly

adj.	季度的
adv.	一季一次地
n.	四分之一、季刊

例 句

It's published quarterly.

這是季刊發行。

衍生單字

☑ quarter *n.* 四分之一、一刻鐘

☞ It's a quarter to three.

還有十五分就三點鐘了。

yearly

adj. 每年的、一年一次的
adv. 每年、年度
n. 年刊

例 句

例 I make a yearly trip to the mountains.
我每年進山一次。

例 Members receive a newsletter twice yearly.
會員每年會收到兩次通訊。

child

n. 孩子、兒童

類似 kid *n.* 孩童

例 句

例 David has a three-year-old child.
大衛有一個三歲的小孩。

相關單字

☑ children *n.* 孩子們（child 的複數）

 track 011

☞ How many children do you have?
你有幾個孩子？

woman

n. 婦女、女人

反義 man *n.* 男性

例 句

例 What a beautiful woman she is!

她真是一位漂亮的女人！

相關單字

☑ women（woman 的複數）

☑ lady *n.* 女性（委婉說法）

folk

n. 人們
adj. 民間的

同義 people *n.* 人們

例 句

例 They are the best folks on the earth.

他們是世界上最好的人。

例 She teaches folk dance in the U.S.A.

她在美國教民族舞蹈。

genius

n. 天才、天賦

例 句

例 Beethoven was a genius.

貝多芬是個天才。

深入分析

1. genius 表示全面的才能,在程度上最高,常指有

天生自發的才能,或具有創造發明的才能。

☞ He showed genius in music from infancy.

他從年幼就顯示了音樂天才。

2. talent是指某特定領域內需要培養和發展的才能。

☞ She has a talent for drawing.

她有繪畫天賦。

3. gift 指某一方面有突出的天賦才能。

☞ His daughter has a gift for art.

他的女兒有藝術的天賦。

graduate

v. 畢業、得學位

n. 畢業生

adj. 畢了業的、研究生的

例 句

例 I graduated from Taiwan University at 22.

我22歲畢業於台灣大學。

track 012

例 He is a medical graduate.

他是大學醫科畢業生。

衍生單字

☑ graduation *n.* 畢業
☑ undergraduate *n.* (未畢業)大學生
☑ postgraduate *n.* 研究生

agency

n. 代理處、代辦處、機構、作用

例 句

例 The company has agencies all over the world.

這家公司在全世界都有代理機構。

dear

adj. 親愛的、寶貴的、昂貴的
n. 親愛的人
int. 唉呀

例 句

例 How are you, my dear friend?

我親愛的朋友你好嗎？

例 Oh, dear! I broke my glasses.

哎呀，我打破了我的眼鏡。

doctor

n. 醫生、博士

例 句

例 "What does he do?" "He's a doctor. "

「他是做什麼的？」「他是醫生。」

例 You'd better see a doctor.

你最好去看醫生。

衍生單字

- ☑ physician   *n.* 內科醫生
- ☑ surgeon   *n.* 外科醫生
- ☑ druggist   *n.* 藥劑師
- ☑ dentist   *n.* 牙科醫生
- ☑ nurse   *n.* 護士
- ☑ patient   *n.* 病人
- ☑ veterinarian   *n.* 獸醫

drug

n. 藥物、麻醉品、毒品
v. 用藥麻醉

例 句

例 The new drug is effective.

這種新藥治療是有效的。

例 They immediately banned the drug.

他們立即取締了這種毒品。

track 013

例 In the hospital he was drugged.

在醫院他接受了麻醉。

medicine

n. 藥、內服藥

例 句

例 Why did you refuse to take the medicine?

你為什麼不肯吃藥？

例 Have you taken your medicine today?

你今天有吃藥了嗎？

衍生單字

☑ pill *n.* 藥丸、藥片

☑ tablet *n.* 藥片

absence

n. 缺席、不在、缺乏、沒有

例 句

例 Look after my house during my absence.

我不在時，要看顧我的房子。

例 I did not notice his absence.

我沒有注意到他的缺席。

衍生單字

☑ absent *adj.* 缺席的

☞ If David is absent from school, he should let me know.

如果大衛沒去學校，他應該要告訴我。

presence

n. 出席、面前

例 句

例 Your presence is requested.

敬請光臨。

例 We shouldn't do it in the presence of my students.

我們不應該在我的學生們面前這麼做。

衍生單字

☑ present *adj.* 出席的

☞ How many people were present at the meeting?

與會的有多少人？

account

n. 說明、理由、報導、帳戶
v. 說明(原因等)

同義 statement *n.* 陳述，說明

 track 014

例 句

例 I have $80 in my checking account.

我的帳戶中有八十元。

例 She opened an account with the bank.

她在銀行開了一個帳戶。

例 I've been asked to account for my conduct.

我被要求對我的行為做出解釋。

track 014

衍生單字

☑ accountant *n.* 會計人員

• justice

| *n.* | 正義、公正、司法、法律制裁 |

| 同義 | integrity *n.* 正直、誠實 |

例 句

例 He expects justice from you.

他希望你能公正地對待。

例 The murderer was brought to justice.

殺人犯已繩之以法。

• horror

| *n.* | 戰慄、恐怖、憎惡、極為恐怖的東西 |

同義	fear *n.* 害怕
	dread *n.* 畏懼、恐怖
	terror *n.* 恐怖、驚駭

例 句

例 The news struck him with horror.

這消息嚇得他毛骨悚然。

例 He has a horror of snakes.

他極憎惡蛇。

衍生單字

☑ horrify v. 使恐怖、使毛骨悚然

☞ The public was horrified by the amount of pollution in the lake.
大眾驚訝湖水的大量污染。

☞ They were horrified at his rudeness.
他們對他的無禮很反感。

• terrify

v. 使害怕、使驚嚇

例 句

例 She was terrified by lightning.
她受到閃電的驚嚇。

例 His looks are enough to terrify anyone.
他的外表足以嚇壞所有人。

衍生單字

☑ terrified n. 受驚嚇的

 track 015

humor

n. 幽默、詼諧

例 句

例 This is a novel full of humor.
這是一部充滿幽默的小說。

例 He has a sense of humor.
他是一個有幽默感的人。

衍生單字

☑ humorous *adj.* 幽默的、詼諧的

disaster

n. 災難、天災、不幸

例 句

例 Over 100 people died in the disaster.
超過百人死於這場災難。

例 All these things were caused by natural disasters.
所有這些事都是自然災害造成的。

衍生單字

☑ financial disaster 金融風暴

☑ disaster aid 災難援助

hire

n. v. 租用、雇用

例 句

例 You ought to hire a lawyer to handle your taxes.
你應該雇用律師來處理你的稅務。

例 These cars are for hire.
這些車輛是供租用。

深入分析

1. hire 用於口語，指短期雇用，臨時雇用某物為自己服務，用物作受詞。

☞ We hired a taxi to take us on a tour of the city.

我們租了一輛計程車作為城市觀光之用。

2. employ 指商店、公司等長期雇用。只用於人,不能用於物。

☞ The men will be employed according to their abilities.

那些人將量才錄用。

3. let 是指租用房屋,或用 rent 也可以。租用設備則用 hire。

☞ This house is to be let, not to be sold.

這間房子只供出租,不出售。

 track 016

fire

v. 解雇

例 句

例 She was fired for stealing from her employer.

她因為偷竊老闆財物被解雇。

例 You are fired.

你被解雇了!

衍生單字

☑ lay off 解雇

☞ The company laid him off last week.

公司上週解雇了他。

culture

n. 文化、文明、教養、修養

例 句

例 Chinese culture has already become widely known in Europe.

在歐洲，中國文化已廣為人知。

例 He is a man of considerable culture.

他是個文化修養很高的人。

衍生單字

☑ cultural *adj.* 文化的、修養的

honor

n. 光榮、榮譽、尊敬
v. 尊敬、給以榮譽

例 句

例 The honor should go to him.

榮譽應歸於他。

例 He won honor for the U.S.A.

他為美國贏得了榮譽。

反義 dishonor *n.* 不名譽、恥辱

衍生單字

☑ honorable *adj.* 高尚的、光榮的

proud

adj. 驕傲的、自豪的、得意的

例 句

例 I am so proud of you.

我以你為榮。

例 She is proud of her accomplishments.

她為自己的成就而自豪。

衍生單字

☑ pride *n.* 驕傲、自尊心

☞ His pride was cut to the quick.

他的自尊心受到極大傷害。

 track 017

error

n. 錯誤、差錯

| 同義 | mistake *n.* 錯誤 |

例 句

例 I showed him his error.

我向他指出了錯誤。

例 He made an error by oversight.

他因疏忽而犯了錯誤。

深入分析

1. error 指漫不經心而出錯，多為筆誤或印刷上、計算上的錯誤。

☞ Please pardon any error that you may discover in my letter.

請原諒我的信中也許有錯誤發生。

2. mistake 指由於缺乏正確的理解或判斷而犯錯誤，程度比 error 輕。

☞ The student's composition is full of mistakes.

這個學生的作文錯誤百出。

3. fault 表示毛病、過失。

☞ It's not your fault.

這不是你的錯。

amount

| n. | 數量、數目、總數 |
| v. | 合計等於、意味著、發展為… |

同義　quantity n. 數量、總量

　　　sum n. 總數、總和

例　句

例 What is the full amount I owe you?

我一共欠你多少錢？

例 His debts amount to $5000.

他的債務共達 5000 元。

sum

| *n.* | 總數、總和、金額 |
| *v.* | 共計、概括 |

| 同義 | amount *n.* 合計、總數 |
| | total *n.* 總數 |

例 句

例 The sum of 5 and 5 is 10.

五加五等於十。

例 It cost an enormous sum.

這花費了一筆鉅款。

例 It sums up to 1,000 dollars.

共計有1000元。

track 018

dollar

| *n.* | （美元）元、一元紙幣、一元硬幣 |

例 句

例 Could you lend me ten dollars?

你可以借給我十元嗎？

例 They spent over one million dollars on the campaign.

他們花了一百多萬美元競選。

相關單字

☑ buck *n.* （美國俚語）元

☞ It cost me five bucks.

這花了我五元。

• data

| n. | 資料、(電腦的)數據 |

例 句

例 The data has been stored in the information bank.

這些資料已被存入資料庫中。

document

| n. | 文件、文獻、公文 |
| v. | 為...提供文件、用文件證明 |

例 句

例 Do you have all your documents in order to apply for a passport?

你有帶齊申請護照的文件嗎？

例 Can you document your claim for compensation?

你能對所要求的賠償提供文件證明嗎？

item

| n. | 專案、條款、項目、一則、一條 |

例 句

例 Please check the items in this bill.

請核對一下帳單中的明細項目。

例 Coffee is the most important export item of Brazil.

咖啡是巴西最重要的出口項目。

temper

n. 脾氣、性情、韌度

| 同義 | emotion *n.* 情緒 |
| | mood *n.* 心情、情緒 |

track 019

例 句

例 David has a bad temper

大衛的脾氣不好！

例 Try to learn to control your temper.

試著控制你的脾氣。

例 They tested the temper of the steel.

他們檢驗了鋼的韌度。

knowledge

n. 知識、學問、見聞、經驗、理解

例 句

例 Knowledge is power.

知識就是力量。

例 He has little knowledge of the fact.

他對實情知道甚少。

• technology

n. 工藝

例 句

例 He's interested in computer technology.

他對電腦科技很有興趣。

science

n. 科學、自然科學

例 句

例 Chemistry, physics, and biology are all sciences.

化學、物理和生物學都是一門科學。

• edit

v. 編輯、校訂、剪輯

例 句

例 He edits the local newspaper.

他負責編輯當地的報紙。

例 He spent all morning editing the book.

他整個上午都在編寫這本書。

衍生單字

☑ editor *n.* 編輯人員

edition

n. 版、版本

例 句

例 This edition is limited to 100 copies.

該版限量推出100本。

track 020

guidance

n. 指引、指導、領導

例 句

例 I need some guidance with my studies.

我學習上需要一些指導。

例 I finished my term paper under the teacher's guidance.

我在老師指導下完成了學期論文。

label

n. 標記、標籤
v. 貼標籤於⋯、把⋯稱為

同義 tag *n.* 標籤、貨籤

例 句

例 He carefully put a label on the box.

他小心地在箱子上貼了個標籤。

例 The bottle had a "poison" label.

瓶子上有「有毒」的標記。

例 He labeled the parcel before posting it.

在郵寄包裹前他貼了標籤。

hell

n. 地獄、苦境

| 反義 | heaven *n.* 天堂 |
| | paradise *n.* 天堂、極樂 |

例 句

例 The priest said they would go to hell for their sins.

神父說他們因罪孽深重要下地獄的。

例 Go to hell!

該死！

lack

n. 缺乏、不足、沒有
v. 缺乏、需要

| 同義 | shortage *n.* 不足 |

例 句

例 She certainly has no lack of friends.

她有很多朋友。

例 They don't lack for funds.

他們不缺資金。

例 I don't seem to lack anything.

我似乎不缺什麼了。

 track 021

laundry

n. 洗衣店、洗好的衣服、待洗的衣服

例 句

例 He runs a laundry.

他開一家洗衣店。

例 Send the shirts to the laundry.

把這些襯衫送到洗衣店去。

例 He picks up the laundry once a week.

他每星期來收一次換洗的衣服。

相關單字

☑ money laundry 洗錢

mission

n. 使命、使團

同義 delegation *n.* 代表團

例 句

例 She was sent on a special mission.

她被派去執行一項特殊使命。

例 The country maintains over 100 missions abroad.

該國在國外設有 100 多個使館。

nationality

n. 國籍、民族

例 句

例 What's your nationality?
你是什麼國籍？

衍生單字

☑ national *adj.* 國家的、民族的、全國的

country

n. 國家、農村、鄉下

例 句

例 China is a country with a long history.
中國是一個歷史悠久的國家。

例 I spent a few days in the country.
我在鄉下住了幾天。

衍生單字

☑ Mainland China *n.* 中國大陸
☑ Japan *n.* 日本
☑ Korea *n.* 韓國
☑ Philippines *n.* 菲律賓
☑ Thailand *n.* 泰國
☑ Myanmar *n.* 緬甸
☑ Indonesia *n.* 印尼
☑ India *n.* 印度
☑ Vietnam *n.* 越南
☑ America *n.* 美國
☑ Canada *n.* 加拿大

 track 022

- ☑ England *n.* 英國
- ☑ Ireland *n.* 愛爾蘭
- ☑ France *n.* 法國
- ☑ Germany *n.* 德國
- ☑ Belgium *n.* 比利時
- ☑ Switzerland *n.* 瑞士
- ☑ Sweden *n.* 瑞典
- ☑ Denmark *n.* 丹麥
- ☑ Italy *n.* 義大利
- ☑ Spain *n.* 西班牙
- ☑ Greece *n.* 希臘
- ☑ Hungary *n.* 匈牙利
- ☑ Norway *n.* 挪威
- ☑ Poland *n.* 波蘭
- ☑ Netherlands *n.* 荷蘭
- ☑ Finland *n.* 芬蘭
- ☑ Russia *n.* 俄國
- ☑ Australia *n.* 澳大利亞
- ☑ New Zealand *n.* 紐西蘭
- ☑ South Africa *n.* 南非
- ☑ Egypt *n.* 埃及
- ☑ Colombia *n.* 哥倫比亞
- ☑ Mexico *n.* 墨西哥
- ☑ Argentina *n.* 阿根廷
- ☑ Brazil *n.* 巴西
- ☑ Panama *n.* 巴拿馬
- ☑ Turkey *n.* 土耳其

navigation

n. 航海術、航行術、航海、航空

例 句

例 He has decided to study navigation.

他已決定學習航海。

例 His navigation of the globe took two years.

他的環球航行花了兩年時間。

property

n. 財產、資產、所有物、性質、特性

例 句

例 He left all his property to his daughter.

他把所有的財產留給了女兒。

例 I confide my property to your care.

我把所有權委託你管理。

例 Many plants have medical properties.

許多植物有藥物特性。

深入分析

1. property 財產，指一切合法的所有物，動產和不動產和各種權力等。

☞ The building is the property of the government.

這座大廈是政府的財產。

2. goods 指動產，指家中或土地上的東西，如家具、工具、設備，不指錢財或文件。

 track 023

☞ Half his goods were stolen.

他的一半財物被盜。

3. effects 指個人的所有物和財產。

☞ His personal effects would be returned to his son.

他個人的財物將歸還給他兒子。

4. fortune 指大筆的財產。

☞ His father left him an immense fortune.

他父親留給他一大筆財產。

5. estate 指傳給子孫後代的不動產。

☞ He divided his estate among his four sons.

他把財產分給四個兒子。

stress

| n. | 壓力、應力、重力 |
| v. | 強調、著重 |

例 句

例 David is under a lot of stress right now.

大衛現在的壓力很大。

例 I stressed that they should not arrive late.

我有強調他們不應該遲到。

role

| n. | 角色、任務、作用 |

例 句

例 She played the leading role in the movie.

她在那部電影中扮演主角。

例 He can play a variety of roles.

他可以演各種不同的角色。

sample

n. 樣品、標本

v. 從...抽樣

同義 specimen *n.* 標本

例 句

例 The doctor took a sample of the patient's blood.

醫生採了這位病人的血液樣本。

例 We sampled the stuff and found it satisfactory.

我們抽查了這種材料,認為滿意。

 track 024

spring

n. 春天、彈簧、彈性、跳躍、泉水

v. 跳、躍

同義 leap v. 跳

bound v. 跳、彈回

例 句

例 It was a beautiful spring day.

這是個天氣很棒的春天氣候。

例 There is not much spring in the old bed.

這張舊床沒多大彈力。

例 The spring has run dry.

這溫泉乾涸了。

衍生單字

- ☑ springy *adj.* 有彈性的、多泉水的

相關單字

- ☑ spring *n.* 春天
- ☑ summer *n.* 夏天
- ☑ autumn=fall *n.* 秋天
- ☑ winter *n.* 冬天

tide

n. 潮、潮汐、趨勢、潮流

同義 current *n.* 潮流

例 句

例 We usually go swimming at low tide.

我們通常在退潮時去游泳。

例 Time and tide wait for no man.

歲月不饒人。

例 The tide of affairs turned in his favor.

形勢變得對他有利起來。

易混淆

- ☑ tide *n.* 潮流
- ☑ tidy *adj.* 整潔的、整齊的

toast

| n. | 烤麵包、祝酒、祝酒辭 |
| v. | 烘、烤、為…敬酒 |

例 句

例 My son likes toast for breakfast.

我兒子早餐喜歡吃烤麵包。

例 Let's drink a toast to our health.

讓我們為健康乾杯。

例 She toasted the bread very dark.

她把麵包烤得很焦。

track 025

trend

| n. | 趨向、趨勢、傾向 |
| v. | 傾向、趨向 |

| 同義 | tendency n. 傾向、趨勢 |

例 句

例 The trend of wages is still upward.

薪資仍有提高的趨勢。

例 Modern life trends towards less formal customs.

現代生活中拘泥於禮節的習俗趨於減少。

深入分析

1. trend指某事物在外界壓力下必然朝著某個方向發展。

track 025

☞ The trend of modern thought is away from idealism.

現代思想有擺脫唯心主義的傾向。

2. tendency 指某人或某物由於自然因素而向一個確定的方向發展，有時指某人特有的習性。

☞ Wood has a tendency to swell if it gets wet.

木材受潮時便會膨脹。

variety

n. 變化、多樣化、品種、變種

例 句

例 My life is full of variety.

我的生活是豐富多姿多彩的。

例 The orchard grows several varieties of apples.

這個果園栽培好幾個品種的蘋果。

例 The shop had a variety of fruit for sale.

這家商店有各種水果出售。

衍生單字

☑ various *adj.* 不同的、各種各樣的

☑ vary *v.* 變化、變更、變異、不同

☑ variation *n.* 變化、變更

welfare

n. 福利

例 句

例 The matter concerns my welfare.

這件事關係到我的福利。

例 They care for the public welfare.

他們關心公共福利。

衍生單字

☑ public welfare *n.* 社會福利

☑ welfare work *n.* 福利事業

track 026

bug

| *n.* | 臭蟲、小毛病、竊聽器 |
| *v.* | 裝竊聽器 |

例 句

例 Some tiny bugs had eaten the leaves of my house plants.

有一些小蟲吃掉我房子種的植物的樹葉了。

例 They planted a bug in the embassy.

他們在大使館放置了竊聽器。

例 The phone has been bugged.

這個電話被竊聽了。

color

| *n.* | 顏色 |

例 句

例 What color is your car?

你的車子是什麼顏色？

track 026

例 What color do you have?

你們有什麼顏色？

例 It comes in many colors.

這個有許多種顏色。

衍生單字

- ☑ black *n.* 黑色
- ☑ white *n.* 白色
- ☑ gray *n.* 灰色
- ☑ silver *n.* 銀色
- ☑ gold *n.* 金色
- ☑ red *n.* 紅色
- ☑ pink *n.* 粉紅色
- ☑ orange *n.* 橙色
- ☑ yellow *n.* 黃色
- ☑ brown *n.* 褐色
- ☑ green *n.* 綠色
- ☑ blue *n.* 藍色
- ☑ purple *n.* 紫色

• food

n. 食物、食品、(精神的)糧食

例 句

例 There were a lot of frozen foods in the refrigerator.

冰箱裡有很多冷凍食品。

例 He has had no food or drink for 24 hours.

他廿四小時沒有進食了！

衍生單字

- ☑ food mixer *n.* 食品攪拌器
- ☑ frozen foods *n.* 冷凍食品
- ☑ sweet foods *n.* 甜食
- ☑ seafood *n.* 海鮮
- ☑ fast food *n.* 速食
- ☑ junk food *n.* 垃圾食物
- ☑ meat *n.* 肉類
- ☑ vegetable *n.* 蔬菜
- ☑ fruit *n.* 水果
- ☑ bakery *n.* 麵包
- ☑ cereal *n.* 穀類

 track 027

meat

n. 食用的肉類

例 句

例 Get a pound of meat from the supermarket on your way home.

你回家的時候順便去超市買一磅的肉回家。

相關單字

- ☑ beef *n.* 牛肉
- ☑ mutton *n.* 羊肉
- ☑ lamb *n.* 小羊肉
- ☑ pork *n.* 豬肉
- ☑ chicken *n.* 雞肉
- ☑ turkey *n.* 火雞肉
- ☑ duck *n.* 鴨肉
- ☑ goose *n.* 鵝肉
- ☑ chop *n.* 排骨

steak

n. 牛排、肉排、魚排

例 句

例 We had beef steak for dinner.

我們晚餐吃牛排。

例 How would you like your steak cooked?

您的牛排要幾分熟？

相關單字

☑ sirloin *n.* 沙朗牛排

medium

adj. (牛排烹調至)五分熟

例 句

例 Would you like your steak rare, medium, or well-done?

你的牛排要煎三分熟、五分熟還是全熟？

例 "How do you like your steak cooked?"

"Well done, please."

「你的牛排要幾分熟？」「全熟。」

相關單字

☑ rare *adj.* (牛排烹調至)三分熟

☑ well-done *adj.* (牛排烹調至)全熟

track 028

fish

n. v. 魚、魚肉、釣魚

例 句

例 We had fish for dinner.

我們晚餐吃魚。

例 We were fishing for salmon last week.

我們上週去釣鮭魚。

例 Let's go fishing.

我們去釣魚吧！

衍生單字

☑ fisher *n.* 漁夫

☑ fisherman *n.* 漁夫

相關單字

☑ cod *n.* 鱈魚

☑ salmon *n.* 鮭魚

☑ shark *n.* 鯊魚

☑ sailfish *n.* 旗魚

☑ sardine *n.* 沙丁魚

☑ cuttlefish *n.* 烏賊

☑ octopus *n.* 章魚

☑ squid *n.* 魷魚、墨魚

clam

n. 蛤蜊、守口如瓶者

例 句

例 Everybody shuts up like a clam as soon as you mention it.

一提及此事，大家便都閉口不言。

相關單字

- ☑ mussel *n.* 蚌類
- ☑ scallop *n.* 扇貝
- ☑ oyster *n.* 牡蠣
- ☑ shrimp *n.* 蝦
- ☑ lobster *n.* 龍蝦
- ☑ crab *n.* 螃蟹

• vegetable

n. 蔬菜

例 句

例 I don't like vegetables.

我不喜歡吃蔬菜。

相關單字

- ☑ cabbage *n.* 包心菜
- ☑ cauliflower *n.* 花椰菜
- ☑ celery *n.* 芹菜
- ☑ lettuce *n.* 萵苣
- ☑ green pepper *n.* 青椒
- ☑ pumpkin *n.* 南瓜
- ☑ eggplant *n.* 茄子
- ☑ pea *n.* 豌豆

track 029

☑ bean *n.* 菜豆
☑ okra *n.* 秋葵
☑ bamboo *n.* 竹筍

track 029

potato

n. 馬鈴薯

例 句

例 I don't like mashed potatoes.
　我不喜歡馬鈴薯泥。

相關單字

☑ potatoes *n.* 馬鈴薯（複數）
☑ couch potato *n.* 電視狂、懶惰的人、整天黏在沙發
　上的人
☞ You are a couch potato.
　你是一個成天窩在沙發上的人。

相關單字

☑ carrot *n.* 紅蘿蔔
☑ radish *n.* 蘿蔔
☑ onion *n.* 洋蔥
☑ potato *n.* 洋芋（複數 potatoes）
☑ sweet potato *n.* 甘薯
☑ taro *n.* 芋頭
☑ beet *n.* 甜菜
☑ beetroot *n.* 甜菜根
☑ corn *n.* 玉米

fruit

n. 水果

例 句

例 We eat a lot of fruits and vegetables at our house.

我們在家裡吃了很多水果和蔬菜。

相關單字

- ☑ apple *n.* 蘋果
- ☑ banana *n.* 香蕉
- ☑ papaya *n.* 木瓜
- ☑ watermelon *n.* 西瓜
- ☑ peach *n.* 桃子(複數 peaches)
- ☑ pear *n.* 梨子
- ☑ date *n.* 棗子
- ☑ guava *n.* 番石榴
- ☑ plum *n.* 李子
- ☑ mango *n.* 芒果(複數 mangoes)
- ☑ orange *n.* 香橙
- ☑ grapefruit *n.* 葡萄柚
- ☑ kiwi *n.* 奇異果
- ☑ walnut *n.* 胡桃
- ☑ almond *n.* 杏仁
- ☑ mulberry *n.* 桑椹
- ☑ chestnut *n.* 栗子
- ☑ pineapple *n.* 鳳梨
- ☑ lemon *n.* 檸檬
- ☑ lime *n.* 萊姆
- ☑ grape *n.* 葡萄
- ☑ strawberry *n.* 草莓
- ☑ cranberry *n.* 蔓越莓
- ☑ blueberry *n.* 藍莓

 track 030

- ☑ cherry *n.* 櫻桃
- ☑ coconut *n.* 椰子
- ☑ sugarcane *n.* 甘蔗

cereal

n. 穀物

例句

例 Do you want cereal or eggs?

你想吃麥片還是蛋？

相關單字

- ☑ rice *n.* 米
- ☑ oat *n.* 燕麥
- ☑ wheat *n.* 麥子
- ☑ oatmeal *n.* 燕麥粥
- ☑ barley *n.* 大麥
- ☑ whole grain rice *n.* 糙米

restaurant

n. 餐廳

例句

例 He invited her to dinner at a French restaurant.

他邀請她去一家法國餐館吃飯。

相關單字

- ☑ hamburger *n.* 漢堡
- ☑ fried chicken *n.* 炸雞
- ☑ chicken nuggets *n.* 雞塊

- ☑ French fries *n.* 薯條
- ☑ hot dog *n.* 熱狗
- ☑ soft drink *n.* 汽水
- ☑ popcorn *n.* 爆米花
- ☑ cola *n.* 可樂
- ☑ coffee *n.* 咖啡
- ☑ large *n.* 大杯(飲料)
- ☑ small *n.* 小杯(飲料)
- ☑ cream *n.* 奶精
- ☑ sugar *n.* 糖
- ☑ ketchup *n.* 蕃茄醬
- ☑ mustard *n.* 芥末醬
- ☑ straw *n.* 吸管
- ☑ paper napkins *n.* 紙巾
- ☑ drinks *n.* 飲料
- ☑ cold drinks *n.* 冷飲
- ☑ beverage *n.* 飲料
- ☑ alcohol *n.* 酒精飲料

quantity

n. 數量

例 句

例 She served each of us a vast quantity of spaghetti.

她盛給我們很多的義大利麵。

 track 031

相關單字

- ☑ **bouquet** *n.* 束

  a bouquet of roses　　　一束玫瑰

  a bouquet of flowers　　一束花

track 031

☑ **box** *n.* 盒裝
  a box of apples   一箱蘋果
☑ **carton** *n.* 硬盒裝
  a carton of orange juice   一盒柳橙汁
  a carton of cigarettes   一盒菸
☑ **can** *n.* 罐裝
  a can of cheese   一罐起司
☑ **bottle** *n.* 瓶
  a bottle of ketchup   一瓶蕃茄醬
☑ **tub** *n.* 塑料杯
  a tub of ice cream   一球冰淇淋
☑ **cup** *n.* 杯子
  a cup of tea   一杯茶
  a cup of coffee   一杯咖啡
☑ **glass** *n.* 玻璃杯子
  a glass of water   一杯水
☑ **dozen** *n.* **12** 個
  a dozen eggs   一打蛋
☑ **ounce** *n.* 盎司
  an ounce of milk   一盎司的牛奶
☑ **pound** *n.* 磅
  a pound of sugar   一磅的砂糖
☑ **liter** *n.* 公升
  a liter of wine   一公升的酒
☑ **quart** *n.* 夸脫
  a quart of oil   一夸脫的油
☑ **gallon** *n.* 加侖
  a gallon of milk   一加侖的牛奶
☑ **loaf** *n.* 條
  a loaf of bread   一條麵包

☑ **bunch** *n.* 串
a bunch of keys　　　　一串鑰匙
a bunch of grapes　　　一串葡萄

☑ **bar** *n.* 長條物
a bar of chocolate　　　一塊條型巧克力

☑ **roll** *n.* 捲狀物
a roll of film　　　　　一捲底片

☑ **stick** *n.* 段
a stick of chewing gum　一段口香糖

☑ **touch** *n.* 一小撮
a touch of salt　　　　一點鹽

☑ **piece** *n.* （紙等的）一張
a piece of paper　　　　一張紙

☑ **pair** *n.* 一對
a pair of scissors　　　一把剪刀
a pair of compasses　　兩個圓規

☑ **clove** *n.* （球類根莖類的）瓣
a clove of garlic　　　　一瓣大蒜

☑ **ball** *n.* 球、團
a ball of wool　　　　　一團毛線

• breakfast

n. 早餐

例 句

例 We had scrambled eggs and toast for breakfast.
我們早餐吃炒蛋和土司。

相關單字

☑ **brunch** *n.* 早午餐

track 032

lunch

n. 午餐

例 句

例 We had soup and sandwiches for lunch.

我們午餐喝湯和三明治。

例 Should we have lunch?

我們要吃午餐了嗎？

dinner

n. 正餐、晚餐

類似 supper *n.* (正式的)晚飯

例 句

例 What's for dinner?

晚餐要吃什麼？

例 Would you like to have dinner with me?

要和我一起吃晚餐嗎？

例 I like to watch TV after dinner.

我喜歡在晚飯後看電視。

supper

n. 正式的晚餐

例 句

例 I usually take a walk after supper.

我通常在晚飯後散步。

例 She has supper on the table.

她準備要吃晚餐了！

track 032

foot

n. 腳、足、英尺

例 句

例 A small house stood at the foot of the mountain.

山腳下有棟小房子。

例 You can get there on foot.

你可以走路過去。

相關單字

☑ feet (foot 的複數)

☞ He's seven feet tall.

他有7英尺高。

 track 033

home

n. 家
adv. 在家地、回家地

例 句

例 He's not at home now.

他現在不在家。

例 On my way home I saw David.

在我回家的路上，我看到了大衛。

Ⓐ Make yourself at home.
請不要拘束。

track 033

house

| n. | 住宅、房子、議院、機構、所、社 |
| v. | 供宿、提供房子居住 |

例 句

Ⓐ We can house you for the weekend.
週末我們可提供你住宿。

相關單字

- ☑ apartment *n.* 公寓
- ☑ suite *n.* 套房
- ☑ flat *n.* 分層的公寓
- ☑ townhouse *n.* 透天房屋
- ☑ building *n.* 建築物
- ☑ dormitory *n.* 宿舍
- ☑ skyscraper *n.* 摩天樓
- ☑ cottage *n.* 農舍別墅
- ☑ farmhouse *n.* 農場住宅
- ☑ country house *n.* 別墅
- ☑ estate *n.* 莊園

desk

| n. | 書桌、辦公桌 |

例 句

Ⓐ There are thirty desks in our classroom.
我們有30張書桌在教室裡。

例 I'm working at my desk.
我正在伏案工作。

相關單字

☑ furniture *n.* 傢俱
☑ table *n.* 桌子
☑ sofa *n.* 沙發
☑ couch *n.* 躺椅
☑ table *n.* 桌子
☑ coffee table *n.* 茶几
☑ stool *n.* 凳子
☑ swivel stool *n.* 旋轉凳子
☑ high chair *n.* 高腳椅
☑ bench *n.* 長椅
☑ footrest *n.* 腳凳
☑ cupboard *n.* 碗櫥
☑ sideboard *n.* 食具櫃
☑ cabinet *n.* 酒櫃　　　　　　　track 033
☑ bookstand *n.* 書架　　　　　　track 034
☑ bookcase *n.* 書櫃
☑ screen *n.* 屏風
☑ shelf *n.* 隔板

•door

n.　門、房門、車門

例 句

例 The door is locked.
門鎖著。

例 Close the door when you leave home.
離開家的時候把門關上。

衍生單字

☑ doorbell *n.* 門鈴

☑ doorman *n.* 看門人

☑ doorstep *n.* 門階梯

☑ doorway *n.* 門口

• garage

n. 車庫、修車廠

例 句

例 I'm looking for a house with a garage.
我在找一間附有車庫的房子。

例 He has taken his car to the garage to have the engine repaired.
他把汽車送到修車廠去修一下引擎。

wall

n. 牆、圍牆

例 句

例 Look at the map on the wall.
看牆上的那幅地圖。

衍生單字

☑ wallpaper *n.* 壁紙

track 034

entry

n. 入口、進入

例 句

例 The entry of the cave was hidden by trees.
洞的入口被樹木掩蓋著。

例 They have the right of free entry to the exhibition.
他們有自由進入展覽會的權利。

place

n. 地方、地點、名次、地位、職位、寓所
v. 安排、任命、放置

例 句

例 This place seems familiar to me.
這地方好像很熟悉。

track 035

例 I took first place in the history examination.
我在歷史考試中得第一名。

例 He has a beautiful place in the country.
他在鄉下有一幢漂亮的房子。

例 I placed their cups on the table.
我把他們的杯子放在桌上。

相關單字

- ☑ city hall　　市政府
- ☑ post office　　郵局
- ☑ station　　車站
- ☑ school　　學校
- ☑ university　　大學
- ☑ library　　圖書館
- ☑ hospital　　醫院
- ☑ pharmacy　　藥局
- ☑ hotel　　旅館
- ☑ theater　　劇院
- ☑ museum　　博物館
- ☑ zoo　　動物園
- ☑ park　　公園
- ☑ church　　教堂
- ☑ station　　車站
- ☑ MRT　　捷運

replace

v. 替換、取代、放回原處

同義	displace *v.* 代替、移置
	substitute *v.* 代替、替換、代理

例 句

例 He was hurt, and another player replaced him.

他受了傷，另一名隊員取代了他。

例 All books must be replaced on the shelves.

所有的書都要放回到書架上去。

深入分析

1. replace 指取代或填補陳舊的、用壞的或遺失的東西。

☞ The capitalist system will replace the socialist system sooner or later.

資本主義制度遲早總要取代社會主義制度。

2. substitute 指一個東西替代另一個東西,在科技上常用。

☞ We should not substitute our personal feelings for the government's policy.

我們不能以個人的感情來代替政府的政策。

track 035

temple

n. 廟宇、神殿、寺院

同義 shrines *n.* 神殿

track 036

例 句

例 They went to the temple for worship.

他們去這座寺廟朝拜了。

bus

n. 公共汽車

例 句

例 We go to school by bus every day.

我們每天坐公共汽車上學。

例 He took a blue bus.

他搭乘了一輛藍色的公共汽車。

track 036

相關單字

☑ buses   (bus 的複數)
☑ car   小汽車
☑ plane   飛機
☑ boat   小船
☑ ship   輪船
☑ train   火車

衍生單字

☑ busboy   *n.* 餐廳打雜者

cycle

| *n.* | 自行車、摩托車、迴圈、周期 |
| *v.* | 騎自行車、騎摩托車 |

例 句

例 She rides on her cycle to work every day.

她每天騎自行車去上班。

例 Do you cycle to school?

你騎自行車上學嗎？

相關單字

☑ bicycle *n.* 腳踏車
☑ motorcycle *n.* 機車

track 036

way

n. 道路、路線、方法、手段

例 句

例 Please show me the way to the shop.

請指引我去商店的路。

例 What is the best way to do it?

做這件事最好的方法是什麼？

例 He usually buys something on his way home.

他通常在回家的路上買東西。

track

v. 跟蹤、追蹤
n. 蹤跡、痕跡、跑道、軌道、徑賽

 track 037

例 句

例 This special scientific instrument is used for tracking planes.

這種特殊的科學儀器是專門用於跟蹤飛機的。

例 The hunter saw the tracks of a deer.

獵人發現了鹿的足蹤。

例 I followed the track through the forest.

我循小路穿過森林。

water

n.	水、雨水、口水
v.	澆水、灑水、供水、滲水

例 句

例 Fish can not live without water.

沒有水魚不能存活。

例 It's very dry; we must water the garden.

天很乾燥，我們得給花園澆水了。

衍生單字

☑ waterfall *n.* 瀑布

☑ watermelon *n.* 西瓜

☑ waterpower *n.* 水力

☑ air *n.* 空氣

☑ soil *n.* 土

name

n.	名字、姓名、名稱
v.	命名

例 句

例 May I have your name, please?

請問你的大名？

例 What's the name of this street?

這條街叫什麼名字？

例 They named the baby Helen.

他們為嬰孩取名為海倫。

無敵**英語單字王**

track 037

brand

| n. | 商標、標記、牌子 |
| v. | 使銘記、打烙印 |

例 句

例 Do you like this brand of coffee?

你喜歡這種牌子的咖啡嗎？

例 He branded the cattle.

他替牛打上烙印。

project

| n. | 方案、計畫、工程、專案 |
| v. | 投射、放映、規劃 |

| 同義 | plan n. 計畫 |
| | scheme n. 計畫 |

track 038

例 句

例 The project was estimated to have cost $100,000.

這項工程估計已耗資十萬元。

例 Will you be able to project the film for us?

你能為我們放映那部電影嗎？

例 Could you project a new working scheme for us?

你能為我們設計一個新的工作計劃嗎？

衍生單字

☑ projector *n.* 放映機、幻燈機、攝影機

nobody

n. pron. 沒有人、誰也不、無足輕重者

例 句

例 Nobody was around to answer the phone.

沒人在附近可以接電話。

例 Nobody could speak Japanese.

沒有人會說日語。

例 There's nobody here.

這裡一個人也沒有。

nothing

n. pron. 沒有東西、沒有什麼

例 句

例 There is nothing good in the evening newspaper.

晚報上沒什麼好消息。

例 We could see nothing but fog.

除了霧，我們什麼都看不見。

例 "Something wrong?" "Nothing."

「有問題嗎？」「沒事！」

anything

pron. 任何事物、一些事物

例 句

例 Are you doing anything tonight?

你今天晚上有事嗎？

例 I won't say anything.

我不會說出任何事的。

例 Do you have anything to say?

你有什麼話要說的嗎?

例 You can't believe anything she says.

她說什麼你都不能相信。

 track 039

someone

pron. 有人、某人

例 句

例 I'm not interested in someone else's experience.

我對其他人的經驗沒有興趣。

例 I'd better ask someone to help me.

我最好請個人來幫我！

something

pron. 某事物

例 句

例 I was anxious to do something.

我做某事會緊張。

例 I was sure something had happened to him.

我確定他發生了一些事。

any

adj. 一些、什麼、任何的
pron. 無論哪個、任何一個

例 句

例 Do you have any black skirts?

你們有賣黑色的裙子嗎？

例 If you have any ideas about it, please tell me.

如果你有任何關於它的想法，請告訴我。

例 Do you have any kids?

你有小孩嗎？

例 Can any of you tell?

你們有誰會說？

anybody

pron. 任何人、無論誰、重要人物

例 句

例 Anybody will tell you where the railway station is.

無論誰都可以告訴你火車站在什麼地方。

例 If you want to be anybody, you must study hard.

如果你想成為重要人物，就須努力學習。

track 039

anyone

pron. 任何人、無論誰

track 040

例 句

例 I didn't know anyone at the party.
我不認識在宴會上的人。

例 Anyone of us has a good family.
我們每個人都有幸福的家庭。

例 Anyone can go. You don't have to be invited.
無論誰都可以去，沒有被邀請也可以去。

thing

n. 事、物、事情、情況

例 句

例 Things will get better soon.
情況很快就會好轉。

例 Put your things away.
把你的東西收拾整齊。

例 Things are more complicated than you thought.
事情比你想像的還要複雜許多。

case

n. 情況、事實、案件、箱

| 同義 | box *n.* 盒子 |

track 040

例 句

例 Don't overstate your case.

不要把你的情況誇大了。

例 Such cases are seldom brought before court.

此類案件很少提交法院處理。

例 The document was kept in a plastic case.

文件放在塑膠盒子裏。

situation

n. 處境、形式、狀況

例 句

例 He's in a difficult situation.

他的處境很艱難。

sake

n. 緣故、理由

| 同義 | purpose *n.* 目的 |

例 句

例 You'd better lock the door for safety's sake.

為了安全起見，你最好把門鎖上。

例 He bought a house in the country for the sake of his wife's health.

為了妻子的健康，他在鄉下買了一幢房子。

 track 041

reason

n. 理由、原因

例 句

例 Is there any particular reason why he doesn't want to come?

他不想來是有特殊原因嗎？

例 He left without giving a reason.

他沒有給任何理由就離開了！

例 That was the reason for telling her.

這就是為什麼要告訴她的原因。

matter

n. 事情、問題、團、塊、堆、麻煩事、毛病
v. 要緊、有關係

例 句

例 You'd better leave the matter in my hands.

你最好把這件事情交給我來處理。

例 What is the matter with the machine?

這機器出了什麼毛病？

例 It doesn't matter now.

現在都不重要了！

occasion

n. 時候、場合、盛會、時機

| 同義 | chance *n.* 機會 |
| | event *n.* 場合 |

track 041

例 句

例 I met her only on one occasion.

我只遇到過她一次。

例 He has had few occasions to speak English.

他很少有機會說英語。

衍生單字

☑ occasional *adj.* 偶爾的

☑ occasionally *adv.* 偶爾地

instance

n. 例子、事例、實例、建議、步驟

| 同義 | example *n.* 例子 |
| | case *n.* 事實、案例 |

例 句

例 There are many instances of good people and good deeds.

好人好事的例子很多。

track 042

例 This is only one instance out of many.
這不過是許多例證中的一個。

例 There are jobs more dangerous than truck driving, for instance, training lions.
還有比駕駛卡車更危險的職業，比如馴獅子。

incident

n. 發生的事

例 句

例 In the future, you must avoid a similar incident.
今後你須避免發生類似事件。

例 She told us about some of the amusing incidents of her holiday.
她告訴我們幾件她假期中遇到的有趣的事。

衍生單字
☑ incidental *adj.* 偶然的

深入分析

1. incident指小事件，也指政治事件或不愉快的事。

☞ Incident often brings out character.
小事情往往可以看出一個人的性格。

2. accident 指事故，如車禍、飛機失事等。

☞ She was killed in a traffic accident.
她死於交通事故。

3. event 指重大事件。

☞ A series of major events took place in 2001.
2001年發生了一連串大事。

track 042

time

n. 時間、鐘點、時光、次數

例 句

例 I don't have so much time.

我沒那麼多時間。

例 What time is it?

幾點鐘了？

例 We had a good time at the party.

我們在派對上很快樂！

例 How many times have you been to Japan?

你去過日本幾次？

clock

n. 時鐘

例 句

例 Something has gone wrong with my clock.

我的鐘壞了。

track 043

o'clock

adv. 點鐘

例 句

例 The time appointed for the meeting was ten o'clock.

指定的開會時間是十點鐘。

例 I'll pick you up at six o'clock.

我六點鐘會來接你。

例 "When do you usually get up?" "At 8 o'clock in the morning."

「你一般是幾點起床？」「早上八點鐘。」

相關單字

☑ second *n.* 秒

☑ minute *n.* 分

☑ hour *n.* 小時

last

n.	最後、死期、最近的東西、持續力
v.	持續、耐久、足夠
adj.	最後的、剛過去的、最近一次的
adv.	最後地、最近地

例 句

例 David was the last to arrive.

大衛是最後一個到達的人。

例 I shouldn't have gone to see a movie last week.

我上星期不應該去看電影。

例 How long will it last?

會維持多久？

track 043

middle

n. 中部、中間、中途

例 句

例 I'm the one in the middle.
我就是中間的那個。

例 I'm in the middle of something.
我正在忙。

moment

n. 一會兒、片刻、瞬間

例 句

例 It'll only take a moment.
這件事只需要片刻的時間。

例 He's busy at the moment.
他現在正在忙。

例 Wait a moment, please.
請稍候。

track 044

second

adj.	第二的
adv.	第二
n.	第二名
n.	秒

track 044

例 句

例 She lives on the second floor.

她住在二樓。

例 Wait a second.

請稍等！

相關單字

☑ first   第一
☑ second   第二
☑ third   第三
☑ fourth   第四
☑ fifth   第五
☑ sixth   第六
☑ seventh   第七
☑ eighth   第八
☑ ninth   第九
☑ tenth   第十

problem

n. 問題、難題

類似 question *n.* 問題

例 句

例 What's your problem?

你的問題是什麼？

例 He'll solve the problem.

他將會解決這個問題。

例 "Do you mind waiting a few minutes?"
"No problem."

「您介意稍等片刻嗎？」「沒問題！」

question

| n. | 問題、質問、論點、疑點 |
| v. | 詢問、審問、對…表示疑問 |

反義 answer *n.* v. 回答

例 句

例 I have one more question.

我還有一個問題。

例 Do you have any questions?

有什麼問題嗎？

例 She's always questioning me about my friends.

她老是質問我朋友的事。

trouble

| n. | 困難、煩惱、麻煩 |

例 句

例 I'm in trouble. Can you help me?

我有麻煩了，你能幫我嗎？

例 I'm sorry for the trouble I'm giving you.

實在抱歉給你添麻煩。

例 You're asking for trouble.

你是在自找麻煩。

衍生單字

☑ troublemaker 麻煩製造者

right

n.	右邊
adj.	右邊的、正確的
adv.	向右地、正確地、完全地、立即地

反義 left *n. adj. adv.* 左、左面、向左

例 句

例 It's on your right side.

在你的右手邊。

例 Is that the right time?

那是正確的時間嗎？

例 I'll be right back.

我馬上就回來。

front

n.	前面、正面
adj.	前面的、最前方的

反義 back *adj.* 背面的

例 句

例 "Where is the post office?" "It's in front of the park."

「郵局在哪裡？」「在公園前面。」

例 The front of the house faces Peach Street.

房子的前方面對著 Peach 街。

例 This is our front garden.

這是我們的前花園。

track 045

衍生單字

- ☑ front door *n.* 前門
- ☑ front line *n.* 最前線、戰線、火線
- ☑ front office *n.* 【美】(公司等的)管理部門、(警察局)總部

side

n. 側面、旁邊、坡、岸、一旁

例　句

例 I have a table by the side of my bed.
我的床旁邊有一張桌子。

 track 046

例 The children sat side by side.
孩子們肩並肩坐著。

decision

n. 決定、決心、果斷

例　句

例 You've made the wrong decision.
你做了一個錯誤的決定。

例 You're the decision maker.
你有決定權。

衍生單字

- ☑ decision tree　　　　決策樹
- ☑ decision maker　　　決策者

exercise

n. 鍛鍊、運動、練習、習題

v. 練習、運動、做體操

例 句

例 If you don't get more exercise you'll get fat.

如果你不多做運動，你就會變胖。

例 How often do you exercise?

你有多常做運動？

例 I'm doing exercises in English grammar.

我正在做英語文法的練習。

experience

n. 經驗、體驗、經歷

例 句

例 I have much experience in teaching English.

我對英語教學有豐富的經驗。

例 Experience is our best teacher.

經驗是我們最好的老師。

例 He gained experience in teaching.

他得到教學經驗。

track 046

fact

n. 事實、真相、事件

例 句

例 The fact is that he's lost his job.

事實是他丟了工作。

例 In fact, I'm sure that's the only satisfactory way out.

事實上，我認為那是唯一令人滿意的出路。

 track 047

truth

n. 事實、實情、實話

反義 lie *n.* 謊言

例 句

例 Tell me the truth.

告訴我實情。

例 I don't know the truth about what happened.

我不知道事情發生的真相。

例 The truth is that I don't know.

事實上是我不知道啊！

motive

n. 動機、目的
adj. 生動的、運動的

例　句

例 The police could not find a motive for the murderer.

警方未能找到謀殺者的動機。

例 Does he have a motive for lying about where he was?

對於他人在哪裡，他有撒謊的動機嗎？

例 Wind is a motive power.

風是一種動力。

favor

n. 恩惠、好意、幫助、贊同

同義 help *n. v.* 幫助

例　句

例 Excuse me, can you do me a favor?

不好意思，你能幫我一個忙嗎？

例 Would you please do me a favor?

可以幫我一個忙嗎？

idea

n. 瞭解、想法、思想、觀念、概念

| 同義 | thought | *n.* | 想法、見解 |

例 句

例 I've got a good idea of what he wants.

他想要什麼我很清楚。

例 I have no idea.

我不知道！

例 "How about going for a walk?"
"Good idea."

「要不要去散散步？」「好主意！」

bath

n. 洗澡、沐浴、浴室、浴缸

例 句

例 Why don't you take a bath?

你何不洗個澡？

例 I often take a cold bath in the morning.

我經常在早上洗冷水澡。

例 I wanna have a bath.

我想洗個澡。

shower

n. 陣雨、淋浴、淋浴間
v. 下陣雨、淋浴

track 048

例 句

例 I take a cold shower every day.

我每天用冷水淋浴。

例 It showered on and off all afternoon.

一整個下午都在下雨！

衍生單字

☑ baby shower 新生兒派對

chance

n. 機會、可能性、偶然、運氣

例 句

例 Don't you think it's a good chance?

你不覺得這是個好機會嗎？

例 We have a good chance of winning the game.

我們很有可能會贏得這場比賽。

例 If you get a chance, come over and see me.

如果有機會的話，來看看我吧！

opportunity

n. 機會

例 句

例 There may be an opportunity for you to see David.

你也許有機會見到大衛一面。

例 She was given the opportunity to manage a day care center.

她被賦予去規劃白天照護中心的機會。

例 He had an opportunity to examine the car.

他有機會去測試這部車。

kind

| adj. | 友好的、和善的 |
| n. | 種類 |

類似　friendly adj. 友好的

例 句

例 It's very kind of you to see me.

謝謝你（們）來看我。

例 Haven't you got any other kinds?

你們沒有別種類型的嗎？

例 This is a kind of rose.

這是一種玫瑰花。

gracious

| adj. | 親切的、客氣的、寬厚的、仁慈的 |

例 句

例 She was gracious enough to show us around her home.

她有禮貌地帶我們參觀她家。

track 049

例 He is kind and gracious to all the sinners who repent.

他對懺悔的人一概慈悲為懷。

sure

adj. 肯定的、確信的

例 句

例 I think so, but I'm not sure.

我是這樣想的，但是我沒有把握。

例 "Are you sure about this?" "Yes, I am."

「這件事你有確定嗎？」「是的，我確定！」

例 I don't know for sure.

我不太清楚。

absolute

adj. 絕對的、完全的

例 句

例 You must tell the absolute truth.

你必須講出全部真相。

例 A child has absolute trust in his mother.

孩子絕對信任自己的母親。

衍生單字

☑ absolutely *adv.* 完全地、絕對地、一點都沒錯

128

track 050

all

adj. 整個的、全部的、所有的
adv. 全部地、完全地
pron. 一切、全部

例 句

例 It's all my fault.

都是我的錯！

例 They were all excited.

他們非常的激動。

例 "Are you busy?" "No, not at all."

「你現在忙嗎？」「不，一點都不忙。」

例 It's all but impossible.

這幾乎是不可能的。

衍生片語

☑ all day 整天
☑ all kinds of 各種各樣的
☑ all one's life 一生、終生
☑ all over 遍及、渾身
☑ all right 可以、好吧、(病) 好了
☑ all the same 仍然
☑ all the time 始終、一直
☑ not at all 一點兒也不

alone

| adj. | 單獨、獨自、獨一無二的 |
| adv. | 僅僅、只、單獨地、獨自 |

例 句

例 Are you alone?

你自己一個人嗎？

例 I'm not alone in this opinion.

不只是我一個人有這個想法。

例 "Are you OK?" "Leave me alone."

「你還好吧？」「不要管我！」

lonely

| adj. | 孤單的、寂寞的 |

例 句

例 When Tracy died, he was very lonely.

崔西死後，他非常孤獨。

例 She gets lonely now that the kids have all left home.

全部的孩子離家後，現在她就非常寂寞。

beautiful

| adj. | 美麗的、漂亮的 |

反義 ugly adj. 醜陋的

track 051

例 句

例 You have a beautiful girl.

你女兒真漂亮！

例 She's so beautiful.

她真是漂亮。

例 It's a beautiful picture, isn't it?

真是一張漂亮的照片，是吧？

衍生單字

☑ beauty *n.* 美麗

big

adj. 大的、長大的

反義 small *adj.* 小的

例 句

例 This is a big house.

這是一座大房子！

例 Do you have any big apples?

你們有賣大顆的蘋果嗎？

例 I'm a big girl.

我已經是大女孩了！

huge

adj. 巨大的、龐大的、非常的

track 051

例 句

例 This is a huge parking lot.

這是一個大型停車場。

例 I spent a huge amount of money on that coat.

我花了大筆的錢買了那件衣服。

例 I have a huge pile of letters to deal with.

我有一大堆信件要處理。

magnificent

adj. 壯麗的、宏偉的、莊嚴的

例 句

例 The view from our room was magnificent.

從我們房間看的景觀是非常宏偉的。

broad

adj. 寬的、廣闊的、廣泛的、寬容的

track 052

例 句

例 His shoulders are very broad.

他的肩膀很寬大。

例 The river grows broader here.

河流在此處變得更寬。

例 The word can only be used in its broad sense.

這個字只能在廣義上使用。

例 He has a broad mind.

他的心胸寬廣。

wide

adj. 寬闊的、寬鬆的、開得很大的、差得遠的

反義 narrow *adj.* 窄的

例 句

例 They came to a wide river.

他們來到了一條寬闊的河邊。

例 The dentist said, "Open wide."

牙醫說:「嘴張大一點」!

tight

adj. 緊貼的、緊的、牢固的、時間緊的

反義 loose *adj.* 鬆的

例 句

例 It's a bit tight.

有點緊。

例 The tight roof kept rain from leaking in.

牢固的屋頂可以防止漏雨。

例 He always has a very tight schedule.

他的行程總是安排得滿滿的。

track 052

衍生單字

- ☑ tightly *adv.* 緊緊地、牢牢地
- ☑ tighten *v.* 使緊、使牢固

loosen

v. 放鬆、鬆開、鬆馳

例 句

📖 He loosened the neck of his shirt.

他鬆開了襯衫的衣領。

📖 Loosen the screw, please.

請把螺絲鬆開。

比 較

- ☑ widen *v.* 加寬
- ☑ sharpen *v.* 削尖
- ☑ broaden *v.* 變闊
- ☑ narrow *adj.* 狹窄的

track 053

release

v. 釋放、解放、發佈、發行、放開、鬆開

同義　free *v.* 使自由、釋放

　　　issue *v.* 發行、發佈

例 句

📖 He was released from jail after two years imprisonment.

他坐了兩年牢之後被釋放出來。

例 The text of the speech was not released until Tuesday afternoon.

演講稿全文到星期二下午才發表。

例 The film has just been released.

這部電影剛剛發行。

例 He released his hold on the rope.

他放手鬆開了繩子。

• vast

adj. 浩渺的、廣大的、鉅額的、大量的

| 同義 | huge *adj.* 巨大的 |
| | immense *adj.* 巨量的、廣大的、巨大的 |

例 句

例 The vast plains spread for hundreds of miles.

這廣闊的平原綿延數百英里。

例 He spent a vast sum of money.

他花去了一大筆錢。

bold

adj. 大膽的、冒失的、粗體(字)的、顯眼的

| 反義 | timid *adj.* 膽小的、怯懦的 |

例 句

track 053

例 A bold attempt is half success.
大膽的嘗試等於成功的一半。

例 She was friendly without being bold.
她友善而不失禮。

例 The headlines are usually printed in bold letters.
標題通常採用粗體印刷。

evident

adj. 明顯的、明白的

| 同義 | apparent *adj.* 明顯的 |

例 句

例 He looked at his son with evident pride.
他帶著明顯的自豪看著他的兒子。

衍生單字

☑ evidently *adv.* 明顯地
☑ evidence *n.* 證據

track 054

easy

adj. 容易的、簡單的、順利的

例 句

例 It's not easy for you.
難為你了！

例 It's not an easy job.
這項工作不簡單！

track 054

例 This one is easier.
這一個比較簡單。

hard

adj. 困難的、硬的
adv. 努力地、猛烈地

例 句

例 It's hard being a single mother.
當單親母親很不容易。

例 The stone was hard.
這岩石很堅硬。

例 It's raining harder than ever.
現在下的雨比任何時候都大。

difficult

adj. 困難的、不簡單的

例 句

例 How difficult it is.
真是困難！

例 It's difficult for me to do so.
要我那樣做是困難的。

衍生單字

☑ difficulty *n.* 困難

track 054

busy

adj. 忙碌的

例 句

例 Are you busy now, Linda?

琳達，妳現在忙嗎？

例 What are you busy with?

你在忙什麼？

例 He's always busy with his work.

他總是忙於工作。

track 055

free

adj. 自由的、空閒的、免費的

例 句

例 "Are you free now?" "Yes. What's up?"

「現在有空嗎？」「有啊！什麼事？」

例 He has little free time.

他很少有空閒的時間。

例 Are the drinks free?

這些飲料是不是免費的？

衍生單字

☑ freedom *n.* 自由

convenience

| *n.* 便利、方便、便利設施 |

例 句

例 We bought this house for its convenience.
我們買這間房子是為了方便。

例 These modern conveniences in the office save them a lot of time.
辦公室的這些現代化便利設備節省了他們許多時間。

衍生單字

☑ convenient *adj.* 方便的、便利的

full

| *adj.* 充滿的、滿的、吃飽的 |

| 反義 empty *adj.* 空虛的 |

例 句

例 I have a full schedule next week.
我下星期行程滿檔。

例 I can't eat any more; I'm full up.
我不能再吃了，我已經飽了。

track 055

hungry

adj. 饑餓的、渴望的

例 句

例 I'm a little hungry.

我有點餓。

例 They're always hungry when they get home from school.

他們放學回家後總是很餓。

衍生單字

☑ hunger *n.* 飢餓

track 056

starve

v. 挨餓、(使)餓死

例 句

例 Because there is no food, people are starving.

由於沒有食物,人們在挨餓。

例 The old man was starved to death.

那老人餓死了。

衍生單字

☑ starvation *n.* 饑餓
☑ starving *adj.* 饑餓的

cheap

adj. 便宜的、廉價品的、不費力的

例 句

例 The bag is very cheap.

這個袋子很便宜。

例 Do you have anything cheaper?

有賣便宜一點的嗎？

expensive

adj. 昂貴的

例 句

例 It's too expensive.

太貴了！

例 Don't you think it's too expensive?

你不覺得太貴了嗎？

dark

adj. 黑暗的、黑色的、深色的

n. 黑暗

反義 bright *adj.* 明亮的

例 句

例 He has dark brown hair.

他有一頭深褐色的頭髮。

track 056

例 They're afraid of the dark.

他們怕黑！

衍生單字

☑ dark horse 黑馬 (表示「出人意外的參賽人」)

each

adj. *adv.* 每個的、各自的、各個的

pron. 每個(物品)、每人、每件(事)

 track 057

例 句

例 "How much is it?" "One hundred each."

「賣多少錢？」「每一個一百元。」

例 Each of the brothers has a different personality.

兄弟每一個人都有不同人格。

every

adj. 每一的、每個的、每隔…的、充分的

例 句

例 Every employee will receive a bonus this year.

今年每位員工都會領到紅利。

例 They're open every day.

他們每天都有營業。

例 I call my parents every two weeks.

我每二週打電話給我父母。

track 057

衍生片語
- ☑ every day 每天
- ☑ every time 每次

• everyone

pron. 每人、人人

例 句

例 You have to wait your turn like everyone else.

你得要和其他人一樣等著輪到你。

例 Is everyone here?

大家都在這裡嗎？

例 Everyone is looking for his book.

大家都在找他的書。

everything

pron. 每件事、每樣東西

例 句

例 I've done everything possible to help you.

我已經盡全力來幫助你了！

例 How is everything?

事情都還好嗎？

例 Come on, everything will be fine.

不要這樣，不會有問題的！

both

adj. adv.	兩個的、一雙的
pron.	兩者、雙方

track 058

例 句

例 I don't know both his parents.
我不認識他的雙親。

例 Would you like milk or sugar or both in your coffee?
你的咖啡裡要加奶精、糖或是兩個都要？

例 Are both of us invited, or just you?
我們兩個人都有被邀請，還是只有你一個人？

far

adj. adv.	（距離或時間的）遠的

反義　close adj. adv. 靠近的、接近的

例 句

例 How far is it from here to Taipei?
從這裡到台北有多遠？

例 It's far away from here.
離這裡很遠。

fast

adj. adv.	快的、迅速的、(鐘錶)偏快的

例 句

㉠ They like fast music.

他們喜歡快節奏的音樂。

㉠ The fastest way to get there is by plane.

到那裡比較快的方式是搭飛機。

㉠ My watch is 5 minutes fast.

我的錶快了五分鐘。

slow

adj. adv. 慢的、緩慢的
v. 放慢速度

例 句

㉠ "Is it fast enough?" "No, it's too slow."

「夠快嗎？」「不，太慢了。」

㉠ He ran slower than the others.

他比其他人跑得還要慢。

㉠ Slow down, honey.

親愛的，慢一點。

• fine

adj. 很好的、健康的、美好的、晴朗的

例 句

㉠ "Hi. How are you?" "Fine, thank you, and you?"

「嗨！你好嗎？」「很好啊，謝謝，你呢？」

track 058

例 We have a fine house.
　我們擁有一棟漂亮的房子。

 track 059

例 It's a fine day, isn't it?
　天氣很好，對吧？

good

adj. 良好的、令人滿意的、愉快的、漂亮的

例 句

例 I am a good singer.
　我是很優秀的歌手。

例 "How do you do?" "Good. How about you?"
　「你好嗎？」「很好。你呢？」

例 It's good to meet you.
　真高興見到你。

well

adj. 健康的
adv. 好、令人滿意地、完全地、充分地
int. 〔表示同意、驚訝〕好、那麼、哎呀

例 句

例 I'm not feeling very well.
　我覺得身體不太舒服。

例 Wash it well before you dry it.
先徹底洗一洗，然後晾乾。

例 Well, all right, I agree.
啊，好吧，我同意。

excellent

adj. 極好的、優秀的

例 句

例 He's excellent in mathematics.
他精通數學。

例 "I did this on my own." "Excellent."
「這是我自己做的！」「很棒啊！」

bad

adj. 壞的、嚴重的、有害的

例 句

例 You're so bad.
你真是壞！

例 It's not bad.
不錯啊！

例 I've got a bad cold.
我得了重感冒。

track 060

awful

adj. 極糟糕的、可怕的、令人不愉快的

| 同義 | dreadful *adj.* 可怕的、令人驚恐的 |
| | horrible *adj.* 可怕的 |

例 句

例 It was an awful film.
這是一部糟糕的電影。

例 I feel awful about it.
我對此感到難過。

例 They took an awful chance.
他們冒著極大的風險。

evil

adj. 邪惡的、壞的
n. 禍害、邪惡、罪惡

| 同義 | bad *adj.* 有害的 |
| | wicked *adj.* 邪惡的 |

例 句

例 He is leading an evil life.
他過著邪惡的生活。

例 The bad man was punished for his evil acts.
這壞人因罪惡的行為而受到懲罰。

例 The love of money is the root of all evil.
貪財是萬惡之源。

track 060

例 The good overbalances the evil.
善良壓倒邪惡。

深入分析

1. evil 指道德上敗壞，語氣強。

☞ It is evil for judges to accept bribes.
法官受賄是罪惡行為。

2. wicked 暗示罪孽深重，常含有幽默、挖苦的含義。

☞ It is wicked of you to torment the poor cat.
你真缺德去折磨那隻可憐的貓。

• guilty

adj. 內疚的、有罪的

例 句

例 She has a guilty look on her face.
她臉上露出了內疚的神色。

例 The judge declared him guilty.
法官判決他有罪。

例 He was guilty of theft.
他犯了盜竊罪。

衍生單字

☑ guiltily *adv.* 有罪地
☑ guiltiness *n.* 有罪、罪惡

innocent

adj. 清白的、天真的、幼稚的、無惡意的

例 句

例 He was innocent of the crime.

他是無罪的。

例 He has an innocent air.

他表現出一種天真的樣子。

illegal

adj. 非法的、不合法的

反義 legal *adj.* 合法的、法律上的

例 句

例 It is illegal to park your car here.

在這裡停車是違法的。

例 He never does anything that is illegal.

他從來不做違法的事。

例 This is an illegal act.

這是一種非法行為。

crime

n. 罪行、愚行、錯誤行為

例 句

例 It is a crime to waste so much food.

浪費那麼多糧食是一種罪過。

Useful English Vocabulary

例 If you commit a crime, you will be punished.

如果你承認犯罪，就會被懲罰。

相關單字

- ☑ criminal *n.* 罪犯
- ☑ prisoner *n.* 囚犯
- ☑ theft *n.* 竊盜
- ☑ murder *n.* 謀殺罪
- ☑ assault *n.* 傷害罪
- ☑ rape *n.* 強姦罪
- ☑ burglary *n.* 半夜闖空門
- ☑ arson *n.* 縱火罪
- ☑ fraud *n.* 詐騙案
- ☑ robbery *n.* 搶劫罪
- ☑ intimidation *n.* 恐嚇罪
- ☑ gambling *n.* 賭博罪
- ☑ sexual harassment *n.* 性騷擾

• rich

adj. 有錢的、含量豐富的、富含油脂的

反義 poor *adj.* 貧窮的

例 句

例 She's a rich woman.

她是一個有錢人。

例 Orange juice is rich in vitamin C.

柳橙汁富含維他命 C。

例 I don't like rich food.
我不喜歡油膩的食物。

poor

adj. 貧窮的、可憐的、缺少的、狀況不好的

例 句

例 He came from a poor, immigrant family.
他來自於一個貧窮的移民家庭。

例 My English is poor.
我的英語不好。

例 The country is poor in natural resources.
這個國家的天然資源不足。

例 He's in very poor health.
他的健康狀況非常不好。

glad

adj. 高興的、樂意的

例 句

例 Glad to meet you.
很高興認識你。

例 I'm glad to hear that.
真高興知道這件事。

例 I'll be glad that you like it.
我很高興你喜歡。

track 062

happy

adj. 高興的、快樂的

反義 sad *adj.* 憂傷的

例 句

例 I'm so happy to hear that.
聽到這件事真高興！

例 She is a happy girl.
她是快樂的女孩！

例 Happy birthday.
生日快樂！（祝福用語）

exciting

adj. 令人興奮的、使人激動的

例 句

例 It's so exciting.
好玩，真是刺激啊！

例 It's an exciting game.
這是場刺激的賽事！

例 This is an exciting story. track 063
這是個很刺激的故事。

sad

adj. 悲傷的、糟透了的、暗淡的

反義　happy *adj.* 快樂的

例 句

例 Don't be so sad.

別這麼難過了。

例 I felt so sad.

我覺得好傷心啊！

例 It's so sad.

真是糟透了！

crazy

adj. 發瘋的、荒唐的、著迷的、狂熱的

同義　mad *adj.* 瘋狂的

例 句

例 You're crazy to go out in this stormy weather.

你真瘋啦，在這樣的暴風雨中出去。

例 She always wears a crazy hat.

她總是戴著稀奇古怪的帽子。

例 She is crazy about jazz.

她對爵士音樂著迷。

track 063

• effective

adj. 有效的、生效的

例 句

例 This medicine is an effective cure for a headache.

這種藥對治療頭疼有效。

例 The agreement will be effective from March 30.

協定從 3 月 30 日起生效。

• neat

adj. 整潔的、利落的、簡潔的

| 同義 | tidy *adj.* 整齊的 |
| | clean *adj.* 乾淨的 |

| 反義 | disorder *adj.* 亂七八糟的 |

例 句

例 Look! How neat the room is!

看，這房間多麼整潔!

例 Cats are neat animals.

貓是愛整潔的動物。

 track 064

例 He was always neat in everything.

他做什麼事都乾淨利落。

衍生單字

☑ neatly *adv.* 整潔地、整齊地
☑ neatness *n.* 整潔

深入分析

1. neat 指清潔、整齊,含有 clean 和 tidy 的意思。

☞ Her clothes are always neat.
她的穿著總是整整潔潔的。

2. tidy 指人習慣上愛整齊,任何東西都安排得井井有
條、不凌亂。

☞ The cottage looked cheerful and tidy.
這幢小屋顯得整齊舒適。

worthy

adj. 值得的、配得上的、可尊敬的、有價值的

例 句

例 David is worthy of praise.
大衛值得稱讚。

例 He is not worthy to be called your son.
他不配被稱為你的兒子。

worth

adj. 有價值的
n. 價值

例 句

例 It's worth it.
真的是物超所值！

stable

adj. 穩定的、安定的、固定的
n. 馬廄

| 同義 | steady *adj.* 穩固的、穩定的 |

| 反義 | unstable *adj.* 不安定的 |

例 句

例 Our country has a stable government.
我國有一個穩定的政府。

例 The groom fed the horses in the stable.
馬夫在馬廄餵馬。

衍生單字

☑ stability *n.* 穩定、穩固搭配
☑ a stable economy 穩定的經濟

track 065

humble

adj.	謙卑的、恭順的、低下的、卑賤的
v.	降低、貶抑

例 句

例 He held a humble position.

他地位低微。

例 Our work was humbled to nothingness.

我們的工作被貶低得一文不值。

衍生單字

☑ humility *n.* 謙遜、謙恭

patient

adj.	有耐心的、能忍耐的
n.	病人、患者

例 句

例 You have to be patient with your mother.

你要對你母親有耐心。

例 He's been a patient of Dr. Smith for many years.

多年來他一直是史密斯醫生的病人。

衍生單字

☑ patience *n.* 耐心

track 065

honesty

n. 誠實、正直、老實

例 句

例 I greatly admire his honesty.

我非常欽佩他的正直。

liar

n. 說謊者

例 句

例 He is anything but a liar.

他不是一個撒謊的人。

wisdom

n. 智慧、明智、名言、格言

例 句

例 People often gain wisdom with age.

智慧往往隨著人的年齡增長而增長。

例 We should learn from the wisdom of our ancestors.

我們應該從祖先的格言中學到教訓。

 track 066

wise

adj. 聰明的、有智慧的

例 句

例 You are wise not to join the club.

你不加入俱樂部是明智的。

例 He's a wise man.

他是聰明的男人。

intelligence

n. 智力、聰明、理解力、情報、消息、報導

例 句

例 Our intelligence shows that the enemy is advancing.

情報表明敵人正在前進。

衍生單字

☑ intelligent *adj.* 聰明的、瞭解的

personal

adj. 個人的、私人的、親自的

| 同義 | individual *adj.* 私人的 |
| | private *adj.* 私人的 |

例 句

例 I keep my personal letters in this box.

我把私人信件收在這個箱子裏。

例 We want to have a personal interview with him.

我們希望與他親自面談。

衍生單字

☑ person　*n.*　人

☑ personally　*adv.*　親自、就個人而論

racial

adj. 人種的、種族的

例 句

例 Their acts of racial oppression must be stopped.

他們的種族壓迫行徑必須停止。

例 He has the racial characteristics of people in Southeast Asia.

他具有東南亞人種的特徵。

衍生單字

☑ race　*n.*　人種、種族

☑ racially　*adv.*　按種族地

☑ racial discrimination　　種族歧視

☑ racial traits　　種族特徵

track 067

passive

adj. 被動的、消極的

| 反義 | active *adj.* 主動的 |

例 句

例 They put the enemy in a passive position.
他們使敵人陷入被動狀態。

衍生單字

☑ passively *adv.* 被動地、消極地
☑ passiveness *n.* 消極、被動

inner

adj. 內部的、裏面的、內心的

| 同義 | internal *adj.* 內部的 |

| 反義 | outer *adj.* 外部的 |

例 句

例 The label is on the inner side of the box.
標籤貼在盒子內側。

例 I was led to an inner room.
我被帶到屋裏。

深入分析

1. inner 指空間的內部或接近中心部分，也用於指思
   想狀態的內心世界。如：inner city 內城區。

track 067

2. inside 主要指空間的意義，有時也指「內幕、內部」的意義，如：inside information 內部消息。

helpful

adj. 有幫助的、肯幫忙的、建設性的

反義 helpless *adj.* 沒有幫助的、無能為力的

例 句

囫 You've been very helpful.

你幫了很大的忙。

衍生單字

☑ helpfulness *n.* 幫助、有益
☑ helpfully *adv.* 有幫助地、有益地

rational

adj. 理性的、合理的

例 句

囫 She was not rational then.

當時她失去了理性。

track 068

potential

adj. 潛在的、可能的
n. 潛力、能力

例 句

例 Education develops potential abilities.

教育能開發人的潛力。

衍生單字

☑ potentially *adv.* 潛在地

responsible

adj. 負責的、承擔責任的、盡責的

例 句

例 Who is responsible for the accident?

誰應對這次事故負責？

例 He is not a responsible person.

他這個人不負責任。

衍生單字

☑ responsibility *n.* 責任

static

adj. 靜的、靜態的

反義 dynamic *adj.* 動的、動力的

例 句

例 Life on campus seemed static, and the students longed for a change.

校園內的生活似乎一成不變，學生們渴望有所改變。

track 068

jealous

adj. 妒忌的、猜疑的

例 句

例 He is jealous of me.

他妒忌我。

例 She was jealous that he had another friend.

她很妒忌他另有一個朋友。

衍生單字

☑ jealousy *n.* 妒忌

☑ jealously *adv.* 妒忌地

envious

adj. 羨慕的、嫉妒的

例 句

例 Do not be envious of your neighbors.

不要羨慕你的鄰居。

track 069

例 She was envious of my successful career.

她嫉妒我的事業成就。

深入分析

1. jealous 指怕失去自己所有的，或想得到他人所有
   的，認為別人所得的東西應屬於自己，因而產生一
   種不滿甚至懷恨的心理。

☞ She is jealous of the better fortune of her roommates.

她妒忌室友的好運。

2. envious「羨慕的、妒忌的」,指對別人獲得的東西,自己很想得到而未得到所產生的情緒。

☞ They are envious of me because I have a good teacher.

他們羨慕我有個好老師。

ridiculous

adj. 可笑的、荒謬的

同義 absurd adj. 可笑的

例 句

例 You look ridiculous in such a dress.

你穿這樣的衣服看上去很可笑。

衍生單字

☑ ridicule v. 嘲笑

☑ ridiculousness n. 荒謬

zealous

adj. 熱心的、熱情的

例 句

例 She is zealous in scientific experiments.

她熱衷於科學實驗。

track 069

junior

adj. 年少的、資歷淺的、等級較低的
n. 年少者、等級較低者、大學三年級學生

例 句

例 Of the two officers, James is the junior.

在這兩個官員中，詹姆斯是下屬。

例 I'm in my junior year.

我正上大學三年級。

相關	freshman 大學一年級生
	sophomore 大學二年級生
	senior 大學四年級生

senior

adj. 年紀較大的、資深的、四年級生的
n. 較年長者

反義	junior *adj.* 較資淺的

例 句

例 He is two years senior to me.

track 070

他比我大兩歲。

例 I'm a senior member of the committee.

我是委員會中的資深委員。

merry

adj. 愉快的、歡樂的

同義	cheerful *adj.* 歡樂的
	delightful *adj.* 令人快樂的
	gay *adj.* 快樂的

例句

例 They wish their friends a merry Christmas.

他們祝朋友們聖誕快樂。

例 Merry Christmas.

聖誕快樂！（聖誕節祝福用語）

衍生單字

☑ merrily *adv.* 愉快地、歡樂地

bare

adj. 赤裸的、空的、勉強的

v. 露出、暴露

同義	naked *adj.* （全身）裸露的

例句

例 They were playing on the beach in bare feet.

他們光著腳在海灘上嬉戲。

例 The house was quite bare.

房子裏空空如也。

例 He earns a bare living by his work.

他的工作僅能維持勉強的生活。

track 070

naked

adj. 光赤的、裸露的、無遮蔽的

| 同義 | bare *adj.* 赤裸的 |

| 反義 | covered *adj.* 遮掩的 |
| | protected *adj.* 遮擋的 |

例 句

例 The children are fighting with naked fists.

孩子們正赤手空拳地打鬥。

例 Many stars can be seen with the naked eye.

很多星星憑肉眼就可以看到。

track 071

prompt

adj. 及時的、迅速的、敏捷的
v. 促使、推動

| 同義 | urge v. 驅策、催促、鼓勵 |

例 句

例 The prompt reply came yesterday morning.

那迅速的答覆是昨天早上到達的。

例 His curiosity prompted him to ask questions.

他的好奇促使他提出問題。

深入分析

1. prompt 意為敏捷的、迅速的、有令人愉悅的感覺。

☞ Deliberate in counsel, prompt in action.

計劃要慎重，行動要果斷。

2. quick 為普通用語、指迅速的，表一瞬間的動作，

時間短。

☞ He has a quick eye and a quick brain.

他眼明心亮。

3. rapid 所指的動作可能是一個，也可能是一連串的。

☞ The patient's pulse was rather rapid.

病人的脈搏跳得相當快。

reliable

adj. 可靠的、確實的

同義 dependable *adj.* 可靠的、可信賴的

例 句

例 Is this information reliable?

這條消息可靠嗎？

例 He is a reliable man.

他是個可信賴的人。

衍生單字

☑ rely *v.* 依賴、依靠

☑ reliability *n.* 可靠性

深入分析

1. reliable 用於人指某人品質和能力都可勝任所需要

的工作，用於物指某物不僅準確而且有用。

track 071

☞ The encyclopedia is a reliable source of information about classical antiquity.

這部百科全書是古代風俗習慣的可靠資訊來源。

2. dependable 用於人指某人很忠誠、沈著,在緊急時刻能信賴、有幫助;用於物指某物能真實可信。

☞ He found the drug dependable.

他覺得這種藥很有幫助。

track 072

normal

adj. 平常的、正常的、正規的

例 句

例 Everything is normal here.

這兒一切正常。

例 What's the normal temperature of the human body?

人體的正常溫度是多少?

衍生單字

☑ normally *adv.* 正常地

深入分析

1. normal 指符合公認的標準、規範或不超過一定的範圍。

☞ He is a normal child in every way.

這孩子各方面均屬正常。

2. regular 指符合某種規則、計劃。

track 072

☞ This is their regular route to the top of the mountain.

這是他們平時登山的路線。

overseas

adv. 在海外、向國外
adj. 海外的、國外的

例 句

例 Overseas trade is important to our country.

海外貿易對我們國家非常重要。

例 The company has three overseas branches.

這家公司有三家海外分公司。

world

n. 世界、地球、宇宙、人世生活

例 句

例 Everest is the highest mountain in the world.

聖母峰是世界最高峰。

例 She has traveled all over the world.

她已經到全世界旅遊過了！

例 The world is round.

地球是圓的。

track 072

例 His whole world fell apart when she left.

當她離開，他的世界就分崩離析了！

universe

n. 宇宙、天地萬物、全世界、全人類

例 句

track 073

例 At that time people believed the earth was the center of the universe.

當時人們相信地球是宇宙的中心。

相關單字

- ☑ Sun *n.* 太陽
- ☑ Mercury *n.* 水星
- ☑ Venus *n.* 金星
- ☑ Earth *n.* 地球
- ☑ Mars *n.* 火星
- ☑ Jupiter *n.* 木星
- ☑ Saturn *n.* 土星
- ☑ Uranus *n.* 天王星
- ☑ Neptune *n.* 海王星
- ☑ Pluto *n.* 冥王星
- ☑ Moon *n.* 月亮
- ☑ star *n.* 星星

army

n. 軍隊、陸軍

track 073

例　句

例 He is in the army.

他在陸軍服役。

相關單字

☑ air force　*n.* 空軍

☑ the army　*n.* 陸軍

☑ the navy　*n.* 海軍

☑ the military　*n.* 軍隊

☑ guerilla　*n.* 游擊隊

☑ task force　*n.* 特遣部隊

☑ general　*n.* 將軍

☑ captain　*n.* 上校

☑ lieutenant colonel　*n.* 中校

☑ major　*n.* 少校

☑ captain　*n.* 上尉

☑ lieutenant　*n.* 中尉

☑ soldier　*n.* 士兵

war

n.　戰爭

例　句

例 They've been at war for the past five years.

過去五年他們都處於戰爭中！

相關單字

☑ civil war　*n.* 內亂

☑ cold war　*n.* 冷戰

☑ hot war　*n.* 熱戰

- ☑ World War   *n.* 世界大戰
- ☑ World War I   *n.* 第一次世界大戰
- ☑ World War II   *n.* 第二次世界大戰
- ☑ nuclear war   *n.* 核子戰爭
- ☑ nuclear weapon   *n.* 核子武器
- ☑ aggression   *n.* 侵略
- ☑ force   *n.* 武力
- ☑ weapon   *n.* 武器
- ☑ offensive   *n.* 攻勢

 track 074

diplomacy

n. 外交、外交手腕

例　句

例 Mr. Brown is highly experienced in international diplomacy.
布朗先生有豐富的國際外交經驗。

相關單字

- ☑ dollar diplomacy   *n.* 金錢外交
- ☑ foreign affairs   *n.* 外交事務
- ☑ power politics   *n.* 武力外交
- ☑ ambassador   *n.* 大使
- ☑ diplomat   *n.* 外交官
- ☑ consul   *n.* 領事
- ☑ embassy   *n.* 大使館
- ☑ diplomatic corps   *n.* 外交使節團
- ☑ diplomatic immunity   *n.* 外交豁免權
- ☑ diplomatic relations   *n.* 外交關係
- ☑ hotline   *n.* 熱線

track 074

education

n. 教育、訓練、受到的教育

例 句

例 More money should be spent on education.

應該將更多的錢應用教育上！

例 She has had a good education.

她受過良好的教育。

衍生單字

☑ educate *v.* 教育

相關單字

☑ educational history *n.* 學歷

☑ educational background *n.* 教育程度

☑ school *n.* 學校

☑ day nursery *n.* 日間托兒所

☑ kindergarten *n.* 幼稚園

☑ infant school *n.* 幼兒學校

☑ primary school *n.* 小學

☑ junior high school *n.* 國中

☑ senior high school *n.* 高中

☑ college *n.* 專科、學院

☑ university *n.* 大學

☑ graduate school *n.* 研究所

☑ study *v. n.* 就學

☑ graduate *v. n.* 畢業

☑ major *n.* 主修

☑ minor *n.* 副修

☑ curriculum *n.* 課程

track 075

exam

n. 考試

| 同義 | examination *n.* 考試 |

例 句

例 I didn't pass my math exam.

我的數學考試不及格！

相關單字

- ☑ pass *n.* 及格
- ☑ fail *n.* 不及格
- ☑ marks *n.* 分數
- ☑ grades *n.* 成績
- ☑ scores *n.* (考試等的)得分

student

n. 學生

例 句

例 David is one of my students.

大衛是我其中的一位學生。

相關單字

- ☑ classmate *n.* 同班同學
- ☑ schoolmate *n.* 同校同學
- ☑ exchange student *n.* 交換學生
- ☑ grade *n.* 年級
- ☑ class *n.* 班級

popular

adj. 流行的、受歡迎的、有名的、走紅的

| 同義 | common *adj.* 大眾的 |
| | ordinary *adj.* 普通的 |

例 句

例 The song is becoming widely popular.

這首歌正廣泛地流行。

例 He is a popular writer.

他是個名作家。

衍生單字

☑ popularly *adv.* 通俗地、一般地

☑ popularity *n.* 通俗性、普及

☑ popularize *v.* 通俗化、大眾化

waterproof

adj. 不透水的、防水的

例 句

例 This cloth is waterproof.

這種布不透水。

例 Put on your waterproof coat before you go out in the rain.

下雨天出門時，要穿防水雨衣。

track 076

opposite

adj. 對面的、對立的
prep. 在……的對面

例 句

例 He lives in the house opposite.

他住在對面的房子裏。

例 He sat down on a sofa opposite to her.

他在她對面的沙發上坐下。

display

v. n. 展覽、陳列、顯示

例 句

例 The boy's suits were displayed in the big window of the store.

男孩的服裝陳列在商場的大櫥窗裏。

例 The local school had two displays of children's drawings.

那所地方學校舉辦過兩次兒童畫展。

深入分析

1. display 著重指公開展示、陳列以供人參觀。

☞ Many flowers were displayed at the flower show.

在花卉展覽上展出了許多花。

2. demonstrate 指不僅給人看，而且還操作表演給人看，並作詳細介紹。

track 076

☞ Please demonstrate how to operate the machine.

請示範表演一下如何操作這個機器。

crash

v. n. 碰撞、墜落、墜毀

例 句

例 The airplane crashed in the hills.

那架飛機在山中墜毀了。

例 He was killed in a car crash.

他死於撞車事故。

例 The dishes fell with a crash.

碟子嘩啦一聲掉在地上。

crush

v. 壓碎、碾碎、鎮壓、壓倒

例 句

例 They crushed the grapes to make wine.

他們把葡萄碾碎用來釀酒。

例 Don't sit on the box. You'll crush it.

別坐在箱子上,你會把它壓壞的。

例 The revolt was crushed.

叛亂被鎮壓下去了。

track 077

深入分析

1. grind 專指碾成粉末狀。

☞ Most of the wheat will be ground into flour.
大部分小麥將被磨成麵粉。

2. smash 指有意或無意地用兇猛的行為突然把某物擊壞或打得粉碎。

☞ He smashed up all the furniture.
他把全部家具都砸爛了。

damage

v. n. 毀壞、損害

| 同義 | harm *v.* 傷害 |

例 句

例 Many of the books were damaged by fire.
許多書被火燒毀了。

例 The cloth damages easily.
這種布容易破損。

例 The earthquake caused great damage.
地震造成了極大的損失。

deserve

v. 應受、值得

例 句

例 Good work deserves good pay.
好的工作應得到好的報酬。

例 He certainly deserved to be sent to prison.

他確實該被送去坐牢。

• shame

n. v. 羞恥、遺憾

例 句

例 It's a shame I haven't heard from you for years.

真遺憾這麼多年沒有你的消息了。

例 What a shame that David couldn't come.

真遺憾大衛不能來！

例 Shame on you.

你真是丟臉！

ashamed

a. 羞恥的、慚愧的、害臊的

例 句

例 You ought to be ashamed of your foolish behavior.

你應該對自己的愚蠢行為感到羞恥。

track 078

amaze

v. 使驚奇、使驚愕、使驚歎

例 句

例 It amazes me how much energy that woman has.

我很驚訝那個女人那麼有精力。

例 It amazed me to hear that you were leaving.

聽到你要走的消息我大吃一驚。

衍生單字

☑ amazing *adj.* 令人驚訝的

☞ It's amazing!

真是令人驚訝！

convince

v. 使確信、使信服

例 句

例 I convinced her that she was mistaken.

我使她相信她是錯誤的。

例 He tried to convince me of his innocence.

他試圖使我相信他是清白的。

衍生單字

☑ convinced *adj.* 有說服力的

track 078

frustrate

v. 挫敗、阻撓、使灰心

例 句

例 The bad weather frustrated our hopes of going out.

壞天氣使我們出門的希望落空了。

例 After two hours' frustrating delay, our train finally arrived.

在兩個小時令人沮喪的延誤之後，我們的火車終於到達了。

contest

v. 爭奪、爭取、競爭、爭辯
n. 競爭、競賽、比賽

同義 competition n. 競爭、比賽

例 句

例 How many people are contesting this seat on the council?

多少人在競爭市議會這個席位？

例 Did you enter the musical contest?

你參加音樂比賽了嗎？

衍生單字

☑ contestant n. 選手、比賽者、爭論者、競選人

track 079

convey

v.　傳送、傳達、運送、輸送

同義　transport v. 運輸、運送

例 句

例 Wires convey electricity from power station to the user.

電線把電從發電廠傳送到用戶。

例 Words can't convey my sorrow.

語言無法傳達我的悲傷。

例 The train conveys goods and passengers.

火車運送貨物和旅客。

衍生單字

☑ conveyance　n.　運送、運輸

☑ conveyer　n.　運送帶、傳送帶

sorry

adj.　難過的、對不起、遺憾的

例 句

例 I feel sorry for you.

我為你感到難過。

例 Sorry for that.

對於那件事真是抱歉！

例 "May I speak to David?" "I'm sorry, but he's on another line."

「我可以和大衛講電話嗎？」「抱歉，但是他正在忙線中。」

greedy

adj. 貪吃的、貪婪的、渴望的

例 句

例 The greedy boy ate up all the cakes.

那個貪吃的孩子把蛋糕全吃光了。

例 He is greedy for knowledge.

他渴望知識。

greet

v. 致敬、迎接

例 句

例 She greeted him with a smile.

她笑著向他打招呼。

例 The view greeted us at the top of the hill.

在山頂上景色盡收眼底。

衍生單字

☑ greeting *n.* 問候、致敬

cold

adj. 寒冷的

n. 寒冷、感冒

反義 hot *adj.* 熱的、炎熱的

例 句

例 It's pretty cold.

很冷喔！

例 It's so cold outside.

外面很冷。

例 I have got a cold.

我感冒了！

hot

adj. 熱的、辣的

例 句

例 It's a hot summer day.

真是炎熱的夏天！

例 I'm too hot in this jacket.

穿夾克真的好熱！

sick

adj. 生病的、厭惡的、噁心的

同義 ill *adj.* 生病的

例 句

例 I'm sick.

我生病了。

例 I'm sick of you.

我對你煩死了！

例 I'm sick of hearing it.
我聽膩那件事了。

• tall

adj. 高的、大的、誇大的

反義 short adj. 矮的

例 句

例 He's seven feet tall.
他有 7 呎高。

例 Is the building tall?
那棟建築物很高嗎?

例 How tall is it?
有多高?

long

adj. 〔距離、時間〕長的、長久的、長形的
adv. 長久地

反義 short adj. 短的

例 句

例 It's a long story.
說來話長。

track 081

例 How long is it?
有多久的時間?

例 Long time no see.
好久不見!

track 081

short

adj. 矮的、短的、短暫的、缺乏的

例 句

例 David is a short boy.

大衛是矮個子的男孩。

例 It's only a short walk to the store.

走路到商店是不遠的。

例 She's short of money this week.

這個星期她的錢不夠用。

衍生單字

☑ shortage　*n.* 短少、不足

☑ shorthand　*n.* 速記

brief

adj. 簡短的、簡潔的

n. 摘要

v. 簡短介紹、簡要彙報

例 句

例 David had a brief career as an actor.

大衛曾經短暫當過演員。

例 Now I give you a brief explanation.

現在我給你作一簡要的解釋。

例 The commander briefed his men.

指揮官向其手下作了指示。

track 081

new

adj. 新的、新鮮的、沒有使用過的、不熟悉的

反義 old *adj.* 舊的

例 句

例 You really need to get a new car.
　你真的需要再買一輛新車。

例 They sell new and used books.
　他們有賣新書和二手書。

 track 082

news

n. 新聞、報導、消息

例 句

例 The news is at nine.
　新聞節目在九點鐘播出。

例 Have you heard any news about your job yet?
　你有聽到關於你的工作的任何消息嗎？

相關單字

☑ advertisement *n.* 廣告
☑ column *n.* 專欄
☑ scandal *n.* 醜聞

old

adj. 年老的、古老的、舊的、…的歲數

反義	young *adj.* 年輕的

類似	elderly *adj.* 年長的

例 句

例 I saw an old lady around here.

我看見附近有一位老太太。

例 There is an old bridge near my home.

我家附近有一座古老的橋。

例 "How old are you?" "I'm twenty years old."

「你多大年紀？」「我廿歲。」

elder

adj.	年齡較大的
n.	年齡較大者

例 句

例 My elder sister is in college.

我姊姊在上大學。

例 He's the elder of two sons.

他是兩個兒子中年齡較大的。

例 I was taught to respect elders.

我被教導要尊重長者。

tender

adj.	嫩的、溫柔的、脆弱的、一觸即痛的

track 082

例 句

例 She was very tender toward the children.

她對待孩子們非常溫柔。

例 The meat is tender.

這種肉鮮嫩。

例 His injured leg is still tender.

他受傷的腿仍然疼痛。

track 083

next

adj. 其次的、緊接著的
adv. 接著、然後、下一步
pron. 下一個

例 句

例 She was next in line after me.

她排隊在我的後面。

例 They're getting married next month.

他們下個月就要結婚了！

例 The next time you want to borrow my dress, ask me first.

如果下次你要借我的衣服，先問我一下！

例 Next, please.

下一位！

衍生片語

☑ next week   下星期

☑ next month   下個月

- ☑ next year 明年
- ☑ next Monday 下個星期一
- ☑ next Tuesday 下個星期二
- ☑ next Wednesday 下個星期三
- ☑ next Thursday 下個星期四
- ☑ next Friday 下個星期五
- ☑ next Saturday 下個星期六
- ☑ next Sunday 下個星期天
- ☑ next time 下次

only

adj. *adv.* 唯一的、僅有的、只是

例 句

例 I'm the only child in my family.
我是家中的獨生子女。

例 It's only five minutes left.
只剩下五分鐘了。

例 "Do you take credit cards?" "Cash only."
「你們收信用卡嗎？」「我們只收現金！」

basic

adj. 基本的

同義 essential *adj.* 基本的、本質的
fundamental *adj.* 基礎的、基本的

例 句

track 083

例 We have to remember the basic vocabulary of a language.

我們必須記住一門語言的基本辭彙。

例 They've received basic training in their native land.

他們在國內接受了基礎訓練。

 track 084

primary

adj. 最初的、首要的、主要的、基本的

同義	elementary adj. 基本的、初級的
	main adj. 主要的
	prime adj. 首要的、最優的、第一流的
	primitive adj. 原始的、早期的、粗糙的

例 句

例 Don't worry. Your illness is still in the primary stage.

別擔心，你的病還在初期。

例 The primary colors are red, blue and yellow.

原色是紅、藍和黃。

衍生單字

☑ a primary organization　基層組織
☑ primary school　　　　小學

ready

adj. 準備好的、隨時待命的

例 句

例 Dinner is ready.

晚餐準備好了！

例 I'm ready. Let's go.

我準備好了。走吧！

例 Are you ready to order?

你要點餐了嗎？

例 I'm not ready for this.

這件事我還沒心裡準備好。

same

adj. 同一的、同樣的
pron. 同樣的人(或事、物)

反義 different *adj.* 不同的

例 句

例 She keeps saying the same thing over and over.

她一直重複說同樣的事。

例 We're all in the same boat.

我們同在一條船上。

例 It's all the same to me.

對我來說都是一樣的。

track 084

different

adj. 不同的、有差異的

例 句

例 Tracy is different from her sister.

崔西和她的姊姊完全不同。

例 We're different, right?

track 085

我們是不同的，對吧？

衍生單字

☑ difference *n.* 不同、差異

some

adj. 某個的、若干的、一些的、好幾個的
pron. 一些、若干、有些人(或事、物)

例 句

例 Can I get some directions?

我能問一下路嗎？

例 Where can I change some money?

我可以在哪裡兌換錢幣？

例 She gave me some advice.

她給了我一些建議。

例 Some of the students are from Taiwan.

有些學生來自台灣。

track 085

many

adj. 許多的（形容可數名詞複數）

n. 許多人(或事、物)

例 句

例 How many would you like?

你要幾個？

例 How many children do you have?

你有幾個小孩？

much

adj. 大量的（形容不可數名詞）

n. 大量的事物

adv. 非常、多

例 句

例 How much sugar do you take in your coffee?

你要在咖啡裡加多少糖？

例 Much of the time was wasted.

許多時間都浪費掉了。

例 Do you dine out much?

你常在外面用餐嗎？

例 Thank you very much.

非常謝謝你！

track 085

few

adj. 不多的、少數的
pron. 少數的人(或事、物)

例 句

例 Do you mind waiting a few minutes?
您介意稍等片刻嗎？

例 He has few good friends.   track 086
他幾乎沒有什麼好朋友。

例 Hurry up! There are few minutes left.
快點！沒有幾多少時間了！

important

adj. 重要的、重大的、地位高的

例 句

例 It's important to me.
對我來說是重要的。

例 Is it really important?
這真的很重要嗎？

例 He is an important player.
他是重要的球員。

例 Do you know how important it is?
你知道這有多重要嗎？

衍生單字

☑ important   *n.* 重要、重要性

track 086

light

n.	光、光線、燈、光源、日光
adj.	輕的、輕鬆的、(顏色)淡的、光亮的
v.	點(火)、點燃、(使)變亮、照亮

例句

例 Plants grow rapidly when exposed to light.

在陽光下的植物生長迅速。

例 This suit is light in color.

這套衣服的**顏色**是淺。

例 Let's light a fire.

我們來生火吧！

衍生單字

☑ lighten *v.* 減輕、(使)輕鬆、(使)發亮、照亮
☑ lighter *n.* 打火機
☑ lighting *n.* 照明、點火
☑ lightning *n.* 閃電

strong

adj.	強壯的、堅強的、濃烈的(飲料等)

反義	weak *adj.* 弱的、虛弱的

例句

例 Is he a strong person?

他人很強壯嗎？

例 He has a strong will.

　　他有堅強的意志。

例 I'd prefer some strong tea.

　　我要濃一點的茶。

wrong

adj. 不對的、錯誤的、不適合的、有問題的

反義　right *adj.* 對的、正確的

例　句

例 There's something wrong with my head.

　　我的頭不太對勁。

例 What's wrong with you?

　　你怎麼啦？

例 Is there anything wrong?

　　有什麼問題嗎？

handy

adj. 方便的、手邊的、近便的

例　句

例 There is a handy place for the telephone.

　　有一個地方很近，打電話很方便。

例 The shops are very handy, only five minutes' walk.

　　這些商店很近，離這兒只要走五分鐘。

track 087

例 I always keep a dictionary handy.

我總是會在手邊放一本字典。

衍生單字

☑ handily *adv.* 輕輕地、便利地

☑ handiness *n.* 近便、便利、靈巧

accurate

adj. 準確的、精確的

| 同義 | correct *adj.* 正確的 |
| | precise *adj.* 精密的、精確的 |

| 反義 | inaccurate *adj.* 不準確的 |

例 句

例 This is an accurate watch; it keeps good time.

這是一隻精確的手錶，時間很準。

例 His information was accurate.

他的情報是準確的。

例 Clocks in railway stations should be accurate.

火車站的時鐘應該非常準確。

angry

adj. n. 憤怒的、生氣的、因為…而生氣

| 同義 | mad *adj.* 發怒的、生氣的 |

track 088

例 句

例 You look so angry.

你看起來好生氣。

例 Don't be so angry, kid.

小朋友，不要這麼生氣！

例 I hope you aren't angry with me.

希望你不要對我生氣！

衍生單字

☑ anger *n.* 生氣

another

adj. 再一、（一群中的）另一、別的、不同的
pron. 另一個、再一個

例 句

例 It'll need another 20 minutes.

還要再廿分鐘。

例 Do you have another solution?

你還有其他解決的辦法嗎？

例 "Would you like to have dinner with me?"
"I'd love to, but I have another plan."

「你要和我一起用晚餐嗎？」「我是很希望去，
但是我有其他計畫了！」

other

adj. (兩者中)另一個的、其餘的、更多的
pron. (兩個中的)另一個人(或物)、其餘的人
(或物)、另一方

track 088

例 句

例 Do you know any other farms?

你知道還有其他農場嗎？

例 I have other plans.

我有其他計畫。

例 Maybe some other time.

那就改天吧！

例 One is mine, another is yours, and the others are his.

一個是我的、有一個是你的、其他都是他的。

familiar

adj. 熟悉的、隨便的、通曉…

反義 strange *adj.* 奇怪的、陌生的

例 句

例 You look so familiar.

你看起來好眼熟喔！

例 I'm familiar with it.

我很熟悉這件事。

例 His name is familiar to all of us. track 089

他的名字我們大家都很熟。

strange

adj. 奇怪的、陌生的、異鄉的 、不可思議的

例 句

例 It's strange we haven't heard from him.
奇怪的是我們沒人知道他的音訊。

例 I'd like to go to a strange area to spend holidays.
我要到異鄉去度假。

| 衍生 stranger n. 陌生人、外地人、外國人 |

深入分析

1. strange「奇怪的」、「對…很生疏的」,指因前所未見而使人感到新奇或不可思議。

☞ That part of town is strange to me.
城鎮的那一部分對我是陌生的。

2. odd「奇怪的」、「古怪的」,用來因一反常態的情況,使人覺得生疏、罕見。

☞ I thought it was odd that they should both have the same opinion.
我認為奇怪的是他們兩人竟有相同的看法。

3. peculiar「奇怪的」、「奇特的」,指所描寫的是顯然不同的、不尋常的或令人困惑不解的任何事物。

☞ He looked at me with a very peculiar expression.
他以十分古怪的表情注視著我。

4. queer「古怪的」、「奇怪的」,指某人故意或因神經不正常而做出的一些離奇可笑的事。

☞ She always speaks in a queer way.
她說話總是怪腔怪調的。

unfamiliar

adj. 不熟悉的、陌生的、不通曉的、未見過的

例 句

例 I saw an unfamiliar face at the door.

我在門口看到一張不熟悉的面孔。

例 I'm unfamiliar with the streets in this neighborhood.

我不熟悉這一帶的街道。

例 I'm unfamiliar with that word.

我不認得那個字。

famous

adj. 著名的、有名的

例 句

例 She's a famous actress.

她是有名的演員。

 track 090

例 Marie Curie is famous for discovering radium.

Marie Curie 對於發現鐳元素享有盛名。

例 The city is famous for its silk.

該市以出產絲綢而聞名於世。

do

aux. v. 做(事)

(*p. pp.*=did; done)

相關 does（do 的第三人稱單數現在式）

例 句

例 I'll do my best to do my work well.

我會盡力做好我的工作。

例 What can I do for you?

我能為你做什麼事？

例 What are you going to do tonight?

你今天晚上要做什麼？

例 How do you do?

你好嗎？

例 She doesn't know how to cook.

她不知道怎麼烹調。

例 I didn't call him last night.

我昨晚沒有打電話給他。

深入分析

do 表示「做(事)」，若是助動詞形式，則有以下
使用規則：

☞ I / we / they ＋ do

☞ David / he / she / it ＋ does

而過去式 did 形態，則適用所有的主詞。

track 090

can

aux. v. 能、會、可以、可能

    (*p.*=could)

例 句

例 Can you do me a favor?

可以幫我一個忙嗎？

例 She can speak French.

她會說法語。

例 You can't play football here.

你不能在這裡踢足球。

深入分析

can 當成名詞，則表示「罐頭」的意思，例如：a can of honey（一罐蜂蜜）。

may

aux. v. 可以、也許、可能、祝、願

例 句

例 May I help you?

要我幫忙嗎？

 track 091

例 May I take a look at it?

我可以看一下這個嗎？

例 Hello, may I speak to John? This is Amy.

哈囉，我能和約翰說話嗎？我是艾咪。

例 May you succeed!

祝你成功！

will

aux. v.	將…、意思、主觀促成、遺贈
n.	遺囑

例 句

例 Will you call him again, please?
可以請你再打電話給他嗎？

例 You will come, won't you?
你會過來，對吧？

例 Do you know when he will be back?
你知道他什麼時候會回來嗎？

例 He willed his house to David.
他立下遺囑，把房子留給大衛。

深入分析

will 同樣具有動詞、助動詞的詞性，可以是「願意
…」、「能夠」、「大概」的意思，但若表示「將
…」，則具有未來的時態，若當成名詞使用，則
是「遺囑」的意思。

must

aux. v.	必須、必定是、堅持要

例 句

例 I must leave at six today.
我必須在今天六點鐘離開。

例 He must have read the letter.
他一定已經看過那封信了。

track 091

例 You mustn't tell anyone about this.

這件事你不能告訴任何人。

go

v.　去、走、通到、達到

(p. pp.=went; gone)

相關　goes（go 的第三人稱單數現在式）

例 句

例 I'd like to go to the museum.

我要去博物館。

例 Let's go home.

我們回家吧！

例 I shouldn't have gone to see a movie last week.

我上星期不應該去看電影。

例 Which road goes to the station?

哪一條路通向車站？

track 092

例 We went to France for our holidays.

我們到法國去度假了。

深入分析

　　go 的變化形使用規則如下：

☞ I / we / they ＋ go

☞ David / he / she / it ＋ goes

　　過去式 went 一樣適用所有的主詞

track 092

come

v. 來、來到

(*p. pp.*=came; come)

| 反義 | go *v.* 去 |

例 句

例 Do you know when he would come back?

你知道他什麼時候會回來嗎？

例 Where do you come from?

你是哪裡人？

例 Here comes my bus. See you later!

我的公車來了。再見囉！

例 I came here from Hong Kong.

我來自香港。

leave

v. 離開、把…留下、委託

(*p. pp.*=left; left)

例 句

例 I must leave now.

我現在要走了。

例 When do you leave for Hong Kong?

你什麼時候要動身去香港？

例 Would you like to leave a message?

你要留言嗎？

track 092

例 My father left a letter for us.

我父親有留一封信給我們。

arrive

v. 到達、抵達

例 句

例 When did you arrive here?

你什麼時候到達這裡的？

例 I've just arrived.

我才剛到。

例 I arrived at the station at ten pm.

我晚上十點鐘抵達車站。

track 093

attend

v. 出席、參加、照顧、護理

例 句

例 If you go out, who will attend to the baby?

如果你出去，誰來照顧孩子？

衍生單字

☑ attendance *n.* 到場、出席

☑ attendant *n.* 服務員、值班員

track 093

attention

n. 注意(力)、留心、立正

例 句

例 The question has aroused considerable attention.

這個問題已經引起相當的注意。

例 He was all attention.

他全神貫注。

例 You should pay more attention to the pronunciation of this word.

你應多注意這個字的發音。

want

v. 要、想要、必要、需要

例 句

例 What do you want for your birthday?

你生日想要什麼禮物？

例 Do you want another drink?

你要再來喝一杯嗎？

例 Everyone wants to attend the concert.

每個人都想參加音樂會。

例 Somebody wants to see you.

有人想見你。

track 093

hand

v.	送、遞給、交付
n.	手、(鐘錶)指針

例 句

例 Please hand me the knife.
請把刀子遞給我。

例 Hand in your paper.
交回你的報告。

track 094

have

v.	有、吃、喝、得到
	(p. pp.=had; had)

例 句

例 Do you have a pencil?
你有鉛筆嗎？

例 What do you want to have?
你想要吃什麼？

例 I had a sandwich for dinner.
我晚餐吃了三明治。

例 May I have your name, please?
請問您的大名？

例 I have to go to New York tomorrow.
我明天得要去紐約。

track 094

get

v.   獲得、成為（某狀態）、到達（某地）
(*p. pp.*=got; got 或 gotten)

例 句

例 How did you get the money?

你是如何弄到這筆錢的？

例 Could you get me a Diet Coke?

請給我低卡可樂好嗎？

例 It's getting dark.

天漸漸黑了。

例 When did you get back?

你什麼時候回來的？

例 Can I get there by bus?

我可以搭乘公車到那裡嗎？

give

v.   給予、付出、舉辦、獻出
(*p. pp.*=gave; given)

例 句

例 Would you give him another chance?

你會再給他另一次機會嗎？

例 I'll give him the message.

我會轉告留言給他。

例 The doctor told me to give up smoking.

醫生要我戒煙。

track 094

make

v.　做、製造、使得、料理
(p. pp.=made; made)

例 句

例 The chairs were made of wood.
椅子是用木頭製造的。

例 What makes you think so?　track 095
你為什麼會這麼想？

例 Make yourself at home.
把這裡當成你自己的家。（不要拘束）

例 Let me make you a sandwich.
我幫你做一個三明治。

衍生單字

☑ maker n. 製造者

happen

v.　碰巧、偶然發生

例 句

例 I happened to be in the neighborhood.
我正好在附近。

例 When did it happen?
是什麼時候發生的？

例 What happened?
發生什麼事了？

track 095

例 What happened to the poor guy?

那個可憐的傢伙發生什麼事了？

change

| v. | 改變、更換、兌換、換穿衣物 |
| n. | 改變、更換、零錢 |

例 句

例 You can change seats with me.

你可以和我交換座位。

例 We changed the date to May 4th.

我們將日期改為五月四日。

例 I've changed my mind.

我改變主意了！

例 She went upstairs to change her clothes.

她上樓去換衣服了。

例 Keep the change.

零錢不用找了！

know

| v. | 知道、認識、懂得、辨別 |
| | (p. pp.=knew; known) |

例 句

例 Do you know when he will be back?

你知道他什麼時候會回來嗎？

track 095

例 I knew it is true.
我就知道那是事實。

例 I've known him for years.
我認識他好幾年了。

track 096

aware

adj. 意識到的、知道的、明白的

例 句

例 He was aware that Tracy would come.
他知道崔西要來。

例 I was quite aware of it before.
我早就意識到這一點了。

hear

v. 聽見、聽說、得知
(*p. pp.*=heard; heard)

例 句

例 Sorry to hear that.
很遺憾知道這件事。

例 What did you hear?
你聽到什麼？

例 I heard something.
我有聽到一些聲音。

track 096

例 I haven't heard from John.

最近我都沒有約翰的消息。

例 I've heard a lot about you.

久仰大名！

listen

v. 仔細聽、傾聽

例 句

例 Listen. Do you hear that?

你聽！有聽見嗎？

例 I listen to the radio every day.

我每天都聽廣播。

例 I didn't listen to what he was saying.

我沒注意聽他在講什麼。

say

v. 說、講、據說
(p. pp.=said; said)

例 句

例 How much did you say?

你說要多少錢？

例 Do you have anything to say?

你有什麼話要說的嗎？

例 He is said to be rich.

據說他很有錢。

track 097

speak

v. 說話、說(某種語言)、提及

(p. pp.=spoke; spoken)

例 句

例 May I speak to David?

我可以和大衛講電話嗎？

例 Can you speak Chinese?

你會說中文嗎？

• talk

v. n. 說、講、聊天、告知

例 句

例 Did you talk to him?

你有和他說過話嗎？

例 We've got to talk.

我們需要談一談。

例 I had a talk with David.

我和大衛談過話了！

tell

v. 告訴、命令、區分

(p. pp.=told; told)

例 句

例 I'll tell David you are here.

我會告訴大衛您到了！

track 097

例 I've told you not to be there.

我有告訴過你不要過去那裡。

例 Can you tell the difference between them?

你分辨得出來他們之間的不同嗎？

distinguish

v. 區別、辨別、辨認出

例 句

例 He is easily distinguished by his uniform.

根據他的制服，很容易把他辨認出來。

mention

n. v. 提及、說起

例 句

例 Don't mention the accident before the children.

別在孩子們面前談到那個事故。

 track 098

例 I enjoyed the meal, not to mention the conversation.

我喜歡那頓飯，至於席上的談話就更不必說了。

例 "Thank you so much." "Don't mention it."

「非常謝謝你！」「不必客氣！」

see

v. 看見、遇見、注意、理解、拜訪

*(p. pp.=*saw; seen)

例 句

例 I saw David going into the station.

我看著大衛走進了火車站。

例 How about seeing a movie?

要不要去看電影？

例 I can't see why it happened.

我不明白為什麼會發生這件事。

衍生單字

☑ seesaw *n.* 蹺蹺板

watch

v. 觀看、注視、看守
n. 手錶、懷錶、小心、看守

例 句

例 Do you often watch TV?

你經常看電視嗎？

例 My watch is 5 minutes fast.

我的錶快了五分鐘！

例 "Watch out." "What? What's wrong?"

「小心點！」「什麼？怎麼啦？」

track 098

look

v.	觀看、注意、好像、顯得、朝著
n.	觀看、臉色、外表

例 句

例 You look terrible.
你看起來遭透了！

例 What are you looking for?
你在找什麼？

例 Look, I know what you're thinking about.
聽好，我知道你在想什麼。

例 Let me have a look at it.
讓我看一下！

travel

v. n. 旅行

例 句

track 099

例 David is travelling in South America.
大衛正在南美洲旅行。

例 I think we should postpone the outing.
我認為我們應該推遲這次郊遊。

例 We had ten day's travel by train.
我們乘火車旅行了十天。

衍生單字

☑ traveler *n.* 旅行者

express

v.	表達、表示
adj.	特快的、快速的
n.	快車

例 句

例 I don't know if I express myself clearly.

我不知道我是否把我的意思表達清楚了。

例 An express train runs up there every morning.

每天早晨都有一趟快速列車開往那裏。

例 My friend and I returned to town by the midnight express.

我和我朋友乘午夜的快車回城。

modify

| *v.* | 修改、更改、修飾 |

同義 alter *v.* 改動

例 句

例 These plans must be modified.

這些計劃必須修改。

例 Adjectives modify nouns.

形容詞修飾名詞。

track 099

衍生單字
☑ modification *n.* 修正、變更
☑ modifier *n.* 修飾語

alter
v. 改變、變更、修改（衣物、計畫等）

例 句
例 We've had to alter our plans.
我們得改變我們的計畫。

例 These clothes must be altered.
這些衣服必須要修改。

 track 100

compare
v. 比較、相比、對比、比作

例 句
例 Shakespeare compared the world to a stage.
莎士比亞把世界比擬為舞臺。

例 Life is often compared to a voyage.
人生常比擬為航海。

boycott
v. n. 杯葛、(聯合)抵制、拒絕參與

例 句

例 They're boycotting the store because the people who work there aren't allowed to join a union.

他們聯合起來抵制那家商店,因為那家商店不允許店員加入工會。

例 They've declared a boycott against foreign goods.

他們聲明聯合抵制外國商品。

bribe

n.	賄賂
v.	向…行賄、買通

例 句

例 The official took bribes from people who wanted favors.

那個官員接受想得到好處的人的賄賂。

例 He couldn't be bribed from the path of virtue.

他不接受誤入歧途的賄賂。

contribute

v.	貢獻、捐助、捐獻、投稿

track 100

例 句

例 Thank you for contributing generously to the relief fund.

感謝你為救濟金慷慨捐助。

例 He contributed widely to publications in many countries.

他向許多國家的出版單位廣泛投稿。

 track 101

donate

v. 捐贈、贈送

例 句

例 He donated a large sum of money from his private purse.

他個人捐助了一大筆錢。

例 Some businesses have agreed to donate computers to schools.

有些企業同意捐贈電腦給學校。

offend

v. 冒犯、觸犯、得罪、使惱火、使不快

例 句

例 She may be offended if you don't reply to her invitation.

如果你對她的邀請不做回應,就可能得罪她。

例 He is offended at my long silence.

他對我長時間的沈默感到惱火。

衍生單字

☑ offense *n.* 罪過、觸犯、冒犯、進攻

cause

v.	引起、使發生
n.	原因、起因、理由

例 句

例 What caused him to quit his job?

是什麼原因使他辭職的？

例 What was the cause of the accident?

造成這個事故的原因是什麼？

• tempt

v.	吸引、引起…的興趣、引誘

同義 attract *v.* 吸引

例 句

例 The cake tempts my appetite.

那塊蛋糕引起我的食欲。

例 His friend tempted him to drink heavily.

他的朋友引誘他酗酒。

例 He tempted me with a bribe.

他用賄賂來引誘我。

track 101

audience

n. 聽/觀眾、會見、拜見

例 句

 track 102

例 The audience consists of 2000 people.

聽眾有2000人。

例 The audience are leaving their seats.

觀眾正離開座位。

enclose

v. 圍住、圈起、封入、附上

例 句

例 The house is enclosed with a high brick wall.

這房子四周圍著一道很高的磚牆。

例 With this letter I enclose a photograph.

隨函附寄一張照片。

衍生單字

☑ enclosure *n.* 包圍、圍繞

emerge

v. 出現、湧現、暴露

例 句

例 Many facts emerged as a result of the investigation.

由於調查，許多事實都暴露出來了。

例 No new ideas emerged during the talks.

會談中沒有出現新意見。

例 The train emerged from the tunnel.

火車從隧道中駛出來。

衍生單字

☑ emergence *n.* 出現

☑ emergency *n.* 緊急情況、不測、危急

weigh

v. 秤重量、重達…

例 句

例 The baby weighed six pounds at birth.

寶寶出生時重六磅。

例 This table weighs a lot.

這張桌子很重。

例 She weighs herself every morning.

她每天量體重。

例 This suitcase weighs a ton.

這件行李非常重。

track 102

深入分析

"weigh a ton"字面意思是「重達一噸」,也就是「非常重」的意思,翻譯的時候可不要只是照字面翻譯喔!

衍生單字

☑ weight *n.* 重量
☑ length *n.* 長度

 track 103

send

v.	送、寄出、派遣、傳遞、迫使
	(*p. pp.*=sent; sent)

反義	receive *v.* 收到

例 句

例 David sent me a birthday card.
　大衛寄給我一張生日賀卡。

例 Some people were sent to help them.
　有一些人被派出去幫助他們。

deliver

v.	遞送、交付、發言

同義	liberate *v.* 解救
	rescue *v.* 解救、救出

例 句

例 We deliver anywhere in the city.

只要是在市內我們都有運送。

例 We had the pizza delivered.

我們點了外送披薩。

例 Would you deliver it to David?

可以把這個送給大衛嗎？

例 I'll deliver a speech at the meeting tomorrow morning.

明天上午我要在會議上發表演說。

衍生單字

☑ deliverance *n.* 解救、釋放、正式意見

☑ deliverer *n.* 救出者、解救者、交付者

☑ delivery *n.* 運送、運送品、交付、陳述、分娩

commit

v. 犯(罪)、做(壞事)、提交、許諾

例 句

例 Two years later he committed suicide.

兩年後他自殺了。

例 They committed the prisoner for trial.

他們把囚犯交付審判。

深入分析

「自殺」的英文可不是"kill me"，而是有特定用法："commit suicide"。

track 103

assign

v. 分配、委派、指定(時間、地點等)

例 句

 track 104

例 He was assigned an important mission.

他分配到一個重要任務。

例 We assigned a day for our meeting.

我們選定一天開會。

衍生單字

☑ assignment *n.* 分配、委派、任務、(課外)作業

bet

n. 打賭、賭注
v. 以…打賭、與…打賭、斷定
　　(*p. pp.*=bet; betted)

例 句

例 The bet was lost.

這賭打輸了。

例 I bet our teacher hasn't come.

我打賭我們的老師現在還未來。

例 I bet she missed the bus.

我打賭她會錯過公車。

track 104

例 David bet me two dollars that he would come.

大衛和我打賭二元認為他會來。

swear

v. 詛咒、咒罵、宣誓、發誓
(*p. pp.*=swore; sworn)

例 句

例 You should not swear in front of the children.

你不該在孩子們面前罵人。

例 He swore to tell the truth.

他發誓已講了實話。

hold

v. 拿著、握住、舉行
(*p. pp.*=held; held)

例 句

例 Could you hold the door open for me?

可以請你幫我扶著門不要關嗎？

例 Could you hold on? I'll just see if he's in.

你不要掛斷好嗎？我去看一看他在不在。

例 We held the meeting on Friday.

我們星期五舉行了會議。

無敵 **英語單字王**

depend

v.	依靠、相信、依賴

例 句

 track 105

例 "When do you leave for Japan?" "It depends on the weather."
「你什麼時候要去日本？」「要視天氣而定。」

例 It depends on your decision.
視你的決定而定。

desire

v.	要求、期望
n.	欲望、要求

例 句

例 They don't really seem to desire change.
他們不是很想要改變。

例 I desire to go home to have a look.
我很想回家去看一看。

例 My desires in life are few.
我生活中的慾望很少。

read

v.	讀、朗讀、察覺
	(p. pp.=read)

例 句

track 105

例 "What are you doing now?" "I'm reading the newspaper."

「你現在在做什麼？」「我正在看報紙。」

例 We read English aloud every morning.

我們每天早上都大聲地朗讀英語。

例 She read my thoughts.

她看出了我的心思。

study

| v. | 學習、研究、細看 |
| n. | 學習、研究、調查、學問 |

同義 learn v. 學習

例 句

例 I've got to study tonight.

我今晚得要唸書。

例 I study Chinese with David.

我和大衛一起學中文。

例 How are you getting along with your studies?

你的研究進展得怎麼樣？

teach

| v. | 教、教書 |
| | (p. pp.=taught; taught) |

反義 learn v. 學習

 track 106

例 句

例 "How did you learn it?" "My father taught me."

「你怎麼學會的？」「我父親教我的。」

例 Can you teach me English?

你可以教我英文嗎？

write

v. 書寫、寫信、填寫、寫下、開罰單
(*p. pp.*=wrote; written)

例 句

例 How often do you write your parents?

你多久寫信給你的父母？

例 He has written some good stories.

他已經寫了一些好的故事。

例 He wrote her a ticket.

他開了一張罰單給她。

衍生單字

☑ writer *n.* 作家

author

n. 作家

例 句

例 Who is the author of this article?

這篇文章的作者是誰？

例 Dickens is one of my favorite authors.

狄更斯是我最喜歡的作家之一。

word

n. 詞、單字、話、談話、申明、通知、諾言

例 句

例 Don't use difficult words.

不要用難懂的字。

例 You have my word.

我向你保證。

詞 組

☑ break one's word　不守諾言、食言
☑ have a word with somebody　和某人說話
☑ in a word　總而言之
☑ in other words　換句話說
☑ word for word　逐字地

• vocabulary

n. 字彙、單字

例 句

例 Reading helps to improve your vocabulary.

閱讀能增進你的單字量。

track 107

witness

n.	目擊者、見證人、證人
v.	目擊、注意到、作證

例 句

例 She was a witness of the accident.

她是這一起事故的目擊者。

例 He witnessed the whole accident.

他目擊了整個事故。

compose

v.	組成、構成、創作、為⋯譜曲

例 句

例 Twelve men compose a jury.

12人組成一個陪審團。

例 He teaches music and also composes music.

他教音樂，還譜寫樂曲。

衍生單字

☑ composer *n.* 作曲家、作者

inquire

v.	調查、查問、詢問、打聽

同義 investigate *v.* 調查、審查

track 107

例 句

例 The police inquired of the deaths of the two girls.

警察調查那兩個女孩的死因。

例 We must inquire into the matter.

我們必須把此事調查清楚。

例 He went to inquire about the times of trains to London.

他去打聽開往倫敦的列車時刻。

evaluate

v.　評定、估價、評價

例 句

例 Doctors evaluate the patient's condition.

醫生評估病人的狀況。

例 Have they evaluated what their next step is?

他們有評估過下一個步驟是什麼嗎？

例 She evaluates people by their clothes.

她根據衣著來評價人。

衍生單字

☑ evaluation *n.* 估價、評價

track 108

survey

n. v. 俯瞰、眺望、全面審視、調查、勘定

例 句

例 Surveys show that 75% of the people approve of the new law.

民意調查顯示，75%的人贊成新頒佈的法規。

例 They have started to survey the country that the new motorway will pass through.

他們已開始測量新公路將穿過的鄉村。

remark

v. 說、評說、就…發表看法、注意、察覺

n. 話語、談論、評論

| 同義 | comment *v.* 評論 |
| | observation *n.* 評語、觀察 |

例 句

例 The editor remarked that the article was well written.

編輯評論說那篇文章寫得很好。

例 In his book there are some interesting remarks on this point.

在他的書裏對這一點有一些有趣的評論。

refer

v. 參考、查閱、查詢、提到、引用、上呈

例 句

例 I referred to my watch for the exact time.
我看了一下手錶好知道準確的時間。

例 Don't refer to this matter again.
不要再提這件事了。

衍生單字

☑ reference n. 提及、涉及、參考、參考書目、
證明書(人)、介紹人

☑ referee n. 裁判

quote

v. 引用、援引、報價

例 句

例 She quoted the Chinese proverb about candles.
她引用了一句關於蠟燭的中國諺語。

例 They quoted a price of $3,000.
他們報的價是3000美元。

例 Is Shakespeare the author most frequently quoted from?
莎士比亞是最常被引用的作家嗎？

 track 109

衍生單字

☑ quotation *n.* 引用、語錄

• relate

v. 與…有關係、使互相聯繫、敘述

例句

例 This is a question that relates to the properties of materials.

這是一個與材料的性質有關的問題。

例 The survey relates high wages to the shortage of labor.

這個調查把高薪資歸咎於勞動力短缺。

例 He related the events of last week.

他敘述了上週發生的事件。

衍生單字

☑ relation *n.* 關係、聯繫

☑ relationship *n.* 關係、聯繫

☑ relative *adj.* 相對的、比較的

• confirm

v. 使更堅固、使更堅定、(進一步)證實確認、批准

同義 prove *v.* 證明

testify *v.* 證明、證實

例 句

例 Your behavior has only confirmed me in my opinion of you.

你的行為反而使我對你的看法更加堅定。

例 They confirmed their hotel booking by phone.

他們用電話再次確定了預訂的旅館。

conform

v. 遵守、依照、符合、順應

例 句

例 You must conform to the rules or leave the school.

你必須遵守規則,不然就離開學校。

例 She refused to conform to the usual woman's role.

她拒絕順應一般婦女該有的角色。

consequence

n. 結果、後果、影響、重要性

例 句

例 Such films can have bad consequences.

這種電影可能會有不良的影響。

track 110

例 The loss of her ring is a matter of great consequence to her.

弄丟戒指對她來說至關重要。

work

v. n. 工作、勞動、運轉、發揮功效

例 句

例 Don't work too hard.

不要工作得太辛苦。

例 You should work out.

你應該要運動身體。

例 I have some work to do tonight.

我今晚有工作要做。

例 It doesn't work.

沒有用的！

深入分析

"work out"可不是在外工作的意思，而是指透過運動健身的意思。

career

n. 生涯、經歷、職業

同義 vocation *n.* 職業、工作

例 句

例 He is getting on well with his career.

他的事業進展順利。

track 110

worry

v. 煩惱、憂慮

例句

例 Don't worry about us.

不要擔心我們！

例 You worry about something.

你有心事！

例 I'm really worried about you.

我真的很擔心你。

annoy

v. 煩惱、打擾

例句

例 He is becoming annoyed with me.

他變得對我厭煩。

例 I was annoyed at the tone of his letter.

我對他信中的語氣感到生氣。

衍生單字

☑ annoyance n. 苦惱、煩人的事物

track 111

forgive

v. 寬恕、原諒

例 句

例 He was forgiven his offences.

他的過錯受到寬恕。

例 Forgive me for interrupting you.

請原諒我打擾你。

例 I'll never forgive you for what you said to me last night.

我永遠不會原諒你昨晚對我說的話。

衍生單字

☑ forgiveness *n.* 寬恕、原諒

☑ forgivable *adj.* 可原諒的、可寬恕的

envy

v.	妒忌、羨慕
n.	妒忌、妒忌的物件、羨慕

例 句

例 I envy your good fortune.

我羨慕你的好運。

例 She is the envy of the town.

她是全城所傾慕的人。

衍生單字

☑ envious *adj.* 羨慕的

深入分析

1. envy 用於貶義，指因未獲得某物而不滿；用於褒義，指希望得到別人得到的東西。

☞ I feel no envy at his success.

我對他的成功毫不妒忌。

track 111

2. jealousy指對別人佔有，企圖佔有應屬於自己的或自己應得的東西而感到不滿或惱恨，甚至懷恨在心。

☞ Susan is full of jealousy of Peter, because she thinks she should have gotten the job instead of him.

蘇珊非常妒忌彼得，因為她覺得她應該得到這份工作而不是他。

apply

v. 申請、請求、致力於、應用

例 句

例 Seven people applied for the position.

有七個人申請這個職位。

例 She applied for a passport.

她申請護照。

例 The rules of safe driving apply to everyone.

安全駕駛規則適用於所有的人。

track 112

appoint

v. 任命、委派、約定

track 112

例 句

例 They appointed him as their representative.

他們委派他為代表。

例 He appointed me to come at one o'clock.

他約我一點鐘來。

衍生單字

☑ appointment *n.* 預約、約會、任命

concern

| *n.* | 關心、掛念、關係、關聯 |
| *v.* | 涉及、有關於、使關心 |

例 句

例 I have no concern in this business.

我與這事無關。

例 It has great concern for us.

此事對我們關係重大。

例 His poor health concerned his parents.

他的身體不好,讓父母很擔心。

accept

| *v.* | 接受、認可 |

例 句

例 Why don't you accept his offer?

你為什麼不接受他的提議?

例 You must accept the fact.

你們必須承認這個事實。

例 I don't want to accept it.

我並不想要接受。

act

v.	行為、表演、扮演、演出
n.	表演、法令、行為

例 句

例 She acted responsibly.

她的行為很得體。

例 He acted as if he'd never seen me before.

他表現得好像從未見過我。

例 He acts the part of Romeo.

他扮演羅密歐這個角色。

track 113

actress

n.	女演員

反義 actor 男演員

例 句

例 What do you do as an actress?

身為女演員，妳都做什麼？

例 He married a beautiful actress.

他娶了一位美麗的女演員。

相關單字
- ☑ waiter *n.* 男服務員
- ☑ waitress *n.* 女服務員
- ☑ steward *n.* 男空服員
- ☑ stewardess *n.* 女空服員
- ☑ lion *n.* 雄獅
- ☑ lioness *n.* 母獅

action
n. 行動、作用

例 句
例 They asked him to reconsider his action.

他們請他重新考慮他的行為。

例 The time has come for action.

行動的時刻到了。

衍生單字
- ☑ bring into action   使行動起來
- ☑ in action   在活動、在運轉
- ☑ take actions   採取行動

admit
v. 承認、允許進入、接納

例 句
例 He admitted having read the letter.

他承認看過那封信。

例 He admitted his guilt.

他承認自己的罪狀。

track 113

例 She admitted that she had made a mistake.
她承認犯了一個錯誤。

• advise

v. 勸告、通知、建議

同義 recommend v. 建議

例 句

例 I advised her that she should wait.
我勸她要等。

例 The doctor advised me to do exercise.
醫生建議我做運動。

衍生單字

☑ advice n. 建議

track 114

recommend

v. 建議

例 句

例 Can you recommend a hotel in Taipei?
你可以推薦在台北的飯店嗎？

例 I recommend that you go on a diet.
我建議你要節食。

衍生單字

☑ recommendation n. 推薦、推薦信、建議、優點

track 114

oblige

v. 迫使、施恩於、幫…的忙、使感激

同義	compel *v.* 迫使
	force *v.* 強迫

例 句

例 I was obliged to leave early to catch my train.

我不得不早走以便趕上火車。

例 I'm obliged to you for your good opinion.

感謝你提的寶貴意見。

衍生單字

☑ obligation *n.* 義務、責任、恩惠、契約

add

v. 增加、補充說明

例 句

例 We've added on a couple of rooms to the house.

我們增加了房子的一些房間數。

例 "I felt sorry for her," added Bob.

「我為她感到惋惜」鮑伯又說道。

衍生單字

☑ addition *n.* 加、附加物

track 114

片語

☑ in addition　另外、加之

☑ in addition to　除…之外

afford

| v. | 擔負得起(……的費用)、抽得出 (時間)、提供 |

例句

track 115

例 I don't know how he can afford a new car.
　　我不知道他怎麼負擔得起一部新車的費用。

例 I can't afford to pay such a price.
　　我付不起這個價錢。

例 I can afford to it.
　　我負擔得起。

例 I'm not sure I could afford the time.
　　我不確定是否抽得出時間。

believe

| v. | 相信、信仰、認為 |

同義　trust v. 相信

例句

例 Believe me. I'm telling the truth.
　　相信我。我說的是實話。

例 You'll never believe what I did.
你不會相信我做了什麼事。

例 Really? I can't believe it.
真的？真不敢相信！

belief

n. 相信、信念、信仰

例 句

例 It is my belief that he will win.
我相信他會贏。

例 It is my firm belief that knowledge is power.
我堅信知識就是力量。

confidence

n. 信任、信心、自信、秘密、機密

例 句

例 I have complete confidence in you.
我完全信任你。

例 They sat in a corner exchanging confidences.
他們坐在角落說著悄悄話。

confident

adj. 有信心的

track 115

例 句

例 They are confident of success.
他們有信心能夠成功。

例 He is confident of passing the examination.
他有信心通過考試。

track 116

doubt

n. v. 懷疑、疑慮

例 句

例 No doubt I'll be in the office tomorrow.
毫無疑問，我明天會在辦公室。

例 I don't doubt that he'll come.
我不懷疑他會來。

例 I doubt if that was what he wanted.
我懷疑那是不是他想要的。

agree

v. 同意、贊同、一致、適合

反義 disagree *v.* 不同意

例 句

例 I don't agree with you.
我不同意。

例 I totally agree to his proposal.
我完全同意他的計畫。

例 I agree with every word you've said.

我同意你説的每一句話。

例 He agreed to get someone to help us.

他同意找人來幫我們的忙。

衍生單字

☑ agreement *n.* 同意

consult

v. 與……商量、請教、查閱

例 句

例 Consult your dictionary when you are unsure of your spelling.

當你不確定拼字時,就查一下詞典。

例 He consulted fully with the masses on each job to be done.

每從事一項工作他都充分地與群眾商量。

approve

v. 贊成、同意、滿意、批准

同義 agree *v.* 同意

反義 disapprove *v.* 不許可,不批准

track 117

例 句

例 My parents approve my becoming a teacher.

我父母贊同我當老師。

例 The company president approved the building plans.

公司總裁批准了建築計畫。

衍生單字

☑ approval *n.* 贊成、同意、認可、批准

testify

v.	説明、證實

(p. pp. ppr. = testified; testified; testifying)

例 句

例 She testified to the innocence of her friend.

她證明了她的朋友無罪。

例 The teacher testified to the pupil's ability.

老師證實了學生的能力。

discuss

v.	討論、商議、詳述

例 句

例 I have to discuss this with you.

我有事情要和你討論。

track 117

例 This booklet discusses how to invest
money wisely.

這本小冊子說明如何聰明投資。

衍生單字

☑ discussion *n.* 討論

yield

v.	出產、生長、屈服、服從
n.	產量、收穫

例 句

例 The beaten army yielded.

被擊潰的軍隊投降。

例 She yielded to her daughter's request.

她同意了女兒的要求。

argue

v.	爭吵、爭辯

同義	persuade *v.* 勸說
	debate *v.* 辯論
	discuss *v.* 討論

例 句

例 They argued about money.

他們對錢的事情爭吵。

track 118

例 I can't argue with you about that.

我同意你。

例 We're always arguing about money.

我們總是為錢爭吵。

例 Do what you are told and don't argue with me.

叫你怎麼做，你就怎麼做，不要和我爭論。

衍生單字

☑ argument *n.* 爭吵

bear

v.	忍受、容忍
	(*p. pp.*=bore; borne)

同義	endure *v.* 忍受、忍耐
	tolerate *v.* 容忍、忍耐

例 句

例 I can't bear that fellow.

我受不了那個傢伙。

例 I couldn't bear it anymore.

我再也受不了了。

例 She bore the pain with great courage.

她以極大勇氣忍受著痛苦。

beat

v.	(連續地)打、敲、拍、(心臟)跳動、戰勝
	(*p. pp.*=beat; beaten)

track 118

例 句

例 We heard the beat of a drum.

我們聽到了擊鼓聲。

例 I hope to beat the record.

我希望能打破記錄。

例 His pulse was still beating.

他的脈搏還在跳動。

hit

v.	擊中、碰撞、遭襲擊、猜對
	(*p. pp. ppr.*=hit; hit; hitting)

例 句

例 Don't hit your little brother!

不要打你弟弟。

例 The ball hit against the window.

球撞擊到窗戶。

例 The area was hit by the floods.

這個地區遭到洪水沖擊。

例 You have hit it.

你猜中了。

track 119

shoot

v.	發射、射擊、掠過、疾馳而過、發芽
n.	嫩枝、苗、射擊、發射
	(*p. pp. ppr.*=shot; shot; shooting)

track 119

例 句

㊽ He shot a bird and killed it.

他打中了一隻鳥並把它打死了。

㊽ Rose bushes shoot again after being cut back.

玫瑰叢修剪後還能再長出新枝。

beg

v. 乞求、請求

(p. pp. ppr.=begged; begged; begging)

例 句

㊽ She begged me not to tell David.

她請求我不要告訴大衛。

㊽ "I beg your pardon?" "I'd like to talk to David."

「你說什麼？」「我要和大衛講電話。」

provide

v. 準備、提供、供給、(法律所)規定

例 句

㊽ The villagers provided the guerrillas with food.

村民們為游擊隊提供食物。

㊽ They worked hard to provide for their large family.

他們努力工作以供養一大家子的人。

衍生單字

☑ provision *n.* 準備、供應、規定

hurry

v. n. 趕緊、急忙

例 句

例 Hurry up. We're late.

快一點！我們遲到了。

例 Don't drive so fast. There is no hurry.

不要把車開得這麼快，沒有必要急急忙忙。

例 I'm in a hurry.

我在趕時間。

例 I'm in a hurry to go home.

我急著要趕回家。

haste

n. 急速、急忙
v. 趕緊、匆忙

同義 hurry *v.* 急忙、匆忙

例 句

例 This work is done with great haste.

這次工作是匆匆忙忙完成的。

track 120

例 I feel no haste to depart.

我不急於離開。

例 In my haste I forgot to lock the door.

我匆忙中忘了鎖門。

衍生單字
☑ hasten v. 趕快
☑ hasty adj. 急忙的、匆忙的
☑ hastily adv. 匆忙地、急忙地

• smile

v. n. 微笑

例 句

例 I couldn't help smiling.

我無法不微笑。

例 When he smiled at me, I knew everything was OK.

當他對我微笑，我就知道事情是沒有問題的。

例 She smiled to herself.

她對著自己微笑。

例 We exchanged smiles as we passed in the hallway.

當在走道上擦身而過時，我們兩人相視而笑。

laugh

v. 笑、嘲笑
n. 笑、笑聲、使人發笑的事

track 120

例 句

例 That guy always makes me laugh.

那個人老是逗我笑。

例 I don't want to be laughed at by my classmates.

我不想被我的同學嘲笑。

cry

v. n. 喊叫、哭、哭聲

例 句

例 A girl is crying for help.

一個女孩子在大聲呼救。

例 The little boy cried out with pain.

這個小男孩疼得大叫。

track 121

例 They were wakened by cries of "Fire!"

他們被「發生火災了」的喊叫聲吵醒。

aid

n. v. 幫助、援助

同義 assistance n. 幫助

track 121

例 句

例 Nurses learn to give first aid to people who are hurt.

護士們學習急救傷患。

例 He came to my aid.

他來幫助我。

例 We aid him with advice.

我們提出意見來幫他。

assist

| v. | 幫助、援助、協助 |
| n. | 幫助（美．口語） |

例 句

例 Two men are assisting the police in their enquires.

有兩個人在協助警方進行對他們的詢問。

例 With the kind assist of her, I have translated the poem into English.

在她的幫助下，我已把這首詩譯成英語。

衍生單字

☑ assistance *n.* 幫助、援助
☑ assistant *n.* 助手
　　　　　 adj. 輔助的、助理的

insult

| n. v. | 侮辱、凌辱、辱罵 |

track 121

同義	despise v. 輕視、蔑視
	scorn v. 蔑視、輕蔑
	indignity n. 侮辱、屈辱

例 句

He was enraged at the insult.

他因受辱而動怒。

He suffered these insults in silence.

他默默承受這些侮辱。

I don't mean to insult you.

我並沒有侮辱你的意思。

live

| v. | 居住、活、生存 |
| adj. | 活著的、現場的、活潑的 |

| 反義 | die v. 死亡 |

例 句

Where do you live?

你住在哪裡？

 track 122

My grandmother lived to be eighty.

我的祖母活到八十歲。

life

| n. | 生物、生命、一生、活力、無期徒刑 |

track 122

例 句

例 There is no life on the moon.

月球上沒有生物。

例 His life was full of misfortunes.

他的一生充滿了不幸。

例 He was sentenced to life.

他被判處無期徒刑。

alive

adj. 活著的、活躍的、熱鬧的

例 句

例 Are your grandparents still alive?

你的祖父母還健在嗎？

例 The city comes alive at night.

這座城市在夜晚是非常熱鬧的。

die

v. 死、滅亡、渴望

(*p. pp. ppr.*=died; died; dying)

例 句

例 David died in 2008.

大衛是 2008 年過世的。

例 He died of a heart attack.

他因為心臟病去世。

track 122

例 He was born in 1990 and died in 2010.

他生於 1990 年，死於 2010 年。

例 My grandfather died 6 years ago.

我爺爺六年前去世了。

例 I'm dying for a cup of coffee.

我好想喝一杯咖啡。

衍生單字

☑ death *n.* 死亡

living

adj. 活的、現存的

n. 生計、生活

例 句

例 There are no living creatures on the moon.

月球上沒有生命。

例 English is a living language.

track 123

英語是現代使用的一種語言。

例 What does he do for a living?

他是靠什麼謀生的？

例 The standard of living in poor countries is very low.

貧窮國家的人民生活水準是很低的。

深入分析

1. live 活的、有生命的、活躍的，僅作定語，只指物，還有「現場直播的」之意。

☞ The laboratory is conducting experiments with a dozen live monkeys.

實驗室正用十二隻活猴子作實驗。

2. **alive** 活著的、活潑的，只作形容詞，特殊情況下作定語要後置。

☞ Despite the hard winter, the rosebush is still alive.

儘管這是嚴冬季節，但月季花叢仍生氣盎然。

3. **living** 既作定語，又作形容詞，活著的，作定語時可前置也可後置。

☞ He is the greatest living novelist.

他是尚健在的最偉大的小說家。

• hang

v. 懸、掛、吊、吊死

例 句

例 Don't hang your coat over here.

不要把你的外套掛在這裡。

例 Will you hang the pictures on the wall?

你把這些畫掛在牆上好嗎？

例 The murderer was caught and hanged.

兇手被捕並被絞死。

例 He hanged himself in his own house.

他吊死在自己家中。

track 123

suspend

v. 懸、掛、吊、暫停、暫緩

例 句

例 A lamp was suspended from the ceiling.

天花板上掛著一盞燈。

例 Bus service was suspended during the strike.

罷工期間公共汽車停止行駛。

moral

adj. 道德上的、道義上的
n. 寓意、教育意義

例 句

例 It's her moral obligation to tell the police what she knows.

她的道德責任讓她告訴警察所知道的事。

track 124

例 The moral of the story is "Look before you leap".

這故事的寓意是「三思而後行」。

衍生單字

☑ morality *n.* 道德、美德

standard

n. 標準、規則
adj. 標準的

例 句

例 The government has an official standard for the purity of silver.

政府對銀的純度有一個正式標準。

例 He speaks standard English.

他講得一口標準的英語。

love

v. 愛、愛戴、喜好、想要
n. 熱愛、愛情、很喜歡、喜愛的事物

反義 hate *v.* 討厭、恨

例 句

例 I don't love him anymore.

我再也不愛他了！

例 Look, you are gonna love this.

聽好，你一定會喜歡這個的。

例 Our love will last forever.

我們的愛情會恆常永久。

hatred

n. 憎惡、憎恨、仇恨

反義 love *n.* 愛、熱愛

例 句

例 He looked at me with hatred.
他用憎恨的眼光看著我。

例 I have a hatred for the miser.
我憎恨小氣的人。

like

v. 喜歡、想要、願意、提出要求
prep. 像、跟…一樣

反義 dislike *v.* 不喜歡

例 句

例 I like your new haircut.
我喜歡你的新髮型。

例 Which one would you like?
你喜歡哪個？

例 I like to go to school by bike. track 125
我喜歡騎自行車去上學。

例 I'd like the chicken soup, please.
我要點雞肉湯，謝謝！

例 Do like this.
就照這樣做。

romantic

adj. 浪漫的、傳奇的、不切實際的、好幻想的

同義 impractical *adj.* 不切實際的、幻想的

例 句

例 David was a romantic poet.
大衛是浪漫派詩人。

例 He is romantic.
他很浪漫。

例 She has a romantic idea of what it's like to be an actor.
她夢想成為女演員。

衍生單字

☑ romance *n.* 羅曼史

likely

adj. 可能的、有希望的
adv. 大概、多半

例 句

例 He is not likely to come.
他很可能不會來。

例 It is likely to be fine.
天氣有希望放晴。

例 He would likely come.
他多半會來。

track 125

probable

adj. 可能性較大的

例 句

例 He thinks that he is a probable candidate.

他認為他是有希望的候選人。

衍生單字

☑ probability *n.* 可能性

深入分析

1. probable 表示主觀上有幾分推測的根據，十有八

九的可能，可能性較大。

☞ He thinks that he is a probable candidate.

他認為他是有希望的候選人。

2. possible 表示客觀上的可能性，又暗示可能性很

小。

☞ I'll do everything possible to help you.

我會盡一切可能幫助你。

track 126

possible

adj. 可能性較小的

例 句

例 Frost is possible, though not probable,
even at the end of May.

即使在五月底，下霜也是可能的，不過可能性不

大。

衍生單字

☑ possibility *n.* 可能性、可能的事

alike

adj. *adv.* 相同的、相像的

例 句

例 We're much alike in character.

我們在性格上非常相似。

例 The children look so alike.

這些孩子們看起來很相似。

例 David treats everyone alike.

大衛對大家一視同仁。

spoil

v. 損壞、破壞、寵壞、溺愛

例 句

例 Try not to spoil any material.

設法別糟蹋材料。

例 They spoil their children.

他們溺愛孩子。

prefer

v. 更喜歡、寧願、提出、呈請

track 126

例 句

例 I prefer to walk there.
我寧願步行去。

例 He prefers walking to riding.
他喜歡步行勝過騎車。

例 He preferred to stay at home rather than go with us.
他寧願留在家裡而不願跟我們一起去。

例 I prefer history to geography.
我喜歡歷史勝過地理。

衍生單字

☑ preferable   *adj.*   更可取的、更合意的
☑ preference   *n.*   更加的喜歡、偏愛、優先(權)

 track 127

disgust

| *n.* | 厭惡、噁心 |
| *v.* | 使厭惡 |

例 句

例 She turned away in disgust.
她厭惡地把臉轉開。

例 I was quite disgusted by his suspicious proceedings.
我十分厭惡他那鬼鬼祟祟的行徑。

preserve

v. 保護、維持、保存、保藏

同義　reserve v. 保存、保留
　　　retain v. 保持、保留

例 句

例 Policemen preserve order in the streets.
警察維持街頭秩序。

例 His work must be preserved for our children and grandchildren.
他的作品必須保存下來留給子孫後代。

衍生單字

☑ preservation n. 保存、保藏

sustain

v. 保持、使…持續、供養、維持

例 句

例 The runner was able to sustain the same pace for hours.
那長跑選手能一連幾小時保持同樣的速度。

例 We had just enough food to sustain us.
我們吃足夠的食物來維持生命。

track 127

process

| n. | 過程、工序、工藝 |
| v. | 加工、處理 |

例 句

It has passed through an interesting process of evolution.

它經歷了一個有趣的進化過程。

It may take a few weeks to process your application.

處理你的申請可能需要幾個星期。

衍生單字

☑ procession *n.* 行列、遊行者

☑ processor *n.* 加工者、處理程式者

track 128

engage

| v. | 從事於、忙著、訂婚、雇用 |

例 句

I don't engage myself in such affairs.

我不參與這種事情。

He is engaged to a pretty girl.

他跟一個漂亮的女孩訂婚了。

He engaged her for the position.

他聘請她擔任這個職務。

divorce

v.	離婚、與…離婚、使分離
n.	離婚

例 句

例 His parents divorced.

他的父母離婚了。

例 Is divorce allowed in that country?

那個國家允許離婚嗎？

refresh

v.	(使)精神振作、(使)精力恢復

例 句

例 He refreshed himself with a cup of coffee.

他喝了杯咖啡提提神。

例 A cold shower will refresh you.

洗個冷水澡會使你恢復精神。

衍生單字

☑ refreshing adj. 令人精神爽快的、提神的

satisfy

v.	滿足、使滿意

例 句

例 Some people are very hard to satisfy.

有些人很難滿足。

track 128

例 He tried to satisfy her every wish.
他千方百計滿足她的一切願望。

例 Nothing satisfies him. He's always com-
plaining.
任何事情都不能使他滿足,他總是在抱怨。

衍生單字
☑ dissatisfy v. 使不滿意
☑ satisfied adj. 滿意的
☑ satisfaction n. 滿意

 track 129

resemble

v. 像、與…相似

例 句

例 They resemble each other in shape.
它們的形狀相似。

例 She strongly resembles her mother.
她特別像她母親。

衍生單字
☑ resemblance n. 相像、相似

resist

v. 抵抗、反抗、忍住、抵制

同義 withstand v. 抵抗、反對

例 句

例 He could hardly resist laughing out loud.
他忍不住放聲大笑。

例 He can not resist sweet foods.
他忍不住想吃甜食。

衍生單字

☑ resistance *n.* 抵抗、反抗、抵抗力、電阻
☑ resistant *adj.* 抵抗的、抗...的、耐...的

resume

| *v.* | 重新開始、繼續、恢復、再用 |

例 句

例 We resumed our journey after a short rest.
我們休息了一會兒之後又重新踏上旅途。

例 He resumed his former position with the company.
他恢復了以前在公司裡的職務。

reward

| *n. v.* | 酬勞、獎賞、報答 |

例 句

例 He received no rewards for his services.
他的服務沒有得到酬謝。

例 He cares little about monetary reward.
他不太關心金錢方面的報答。

track 129

forget

v.	忘記、忘記帶(或買)、放棄
	(*p. pp.*=forgot; forgotten)

反義 remember *v.* 記得

例 句

 track 130

例 You'd better not forget your mother's birthday.

你最好不要忘記你母親的生日。

例 She forgot that she had a dental appointment.

她忘記和牙醫有約了。

例 Don't forget to lock the car.

不要忘記鎖車門。

例 I wish I could forget him but I can't.

我希望我能忘掉他,但是我忘不掉。

例 "Let's go to a movie tonight." "Forget about it. I've got too much work to do."

「我們今晚去看電影吧!」「算了啦!我有好多工作要做。」

remember

v.	記得、想起、回憶起、記住、代…問好

同義 recall *v.* 記得、回憶起

track 130

例 句

例 Remember to buy some stamps.

記得要去買一些郵票。

例 I can't remember how to get there.

我想不起是怎麼到那裡的。

例 Can you remember where we parked the car?

你記得我們把車子停在哪裡了嗎？

• remind

v. 提醒、使想起

例 句

例 Be sure to remind her to come back early.

一定要提醒她早點回來。

例 That reminds me of a short story by Mark Twain.

這使我想起馬克吐温寫的一個短篇小說。

衍生單字

☑ reminder *n.* 提示、提醒者、提醒物

overlook

v. 俯瞰、眺望、遺漏、忽略、寬容

| 同義 | neglect *v.* 忽視 |
| | disregard *v.* 忽視 |

track 130

例句

⑩ The house overlooks the village.
　山上的房屋可俯瞰那座村莊。

track 131

⑩ You have overlooked several of the mistakes in this book.
　你漏看了這本書中的幾處錯誤。

⑩ I'll overlook it this time, but don't do it again.
　這次我寬容你，但下不為例。

•ignore

v. 不理、忽略

例句

⑩ He ignored the doctor's advice.
　他不顧醫生的警告。

⑩ Never ignore the law.
　不要忽視法律。

⑩ We can not ignore such provocation.
　對這種挑釁，我們不能置之不理。

深入分析

1. ignore 指有意置之不理。

☞ He ignored the speed limit and drove very fast.
　他不顧時速限制，開車很快。

track 131

2. neglect 由於疏忽大意或不在意，忘記忽略。

☞ Don't neglect to write to your mother.
別忘了給你媽媽寫信。

3. overlook 指粗心或匆忙中的疏忽，不經意漏掉。

☞ These little details are easily overlooked.
這些小細節很容易被忽略掉。

trick

v. 欺詐、哄騙

n. 戲法、技巧、花招

同義 | cheat v. 欺騙

例 句

例 He was tricked into buying a poor bicycle.
他受騙買了輛品質差的自行車。

例 His father taught him the tricks of trade.
他父親教他做生意的秘訣。

pursue

v. 追趕、追蹤、追求、從事

同義 | tail v. 追隨
trail v. 跟蹤
chase v. 追逐
follow v. 跟隨

例 句

例 He pursued the river to its source.
他沿著河流走到源頭。

track 131

例 The police are pursuing an escaped
prisoner.

警察正在追捕一名逃犯。

 track 132

例 The police pursued on foot, but lost him in
the crowd.

警察徒步追趕，卻在人群中跟丟了。

例 The police are pursuing after a fugitive.

警察在追捕一名逃犯。

衍生單字

☑ pursuer *n.* 追求者、從事者
☑ pursuit *n.* 追趕、追求

qualify

v. 使有資格、使勝任

例 句

例 His training qualifies him as a teacher of
English.

他所受的訓練使他有資格擔任英語教師。

例 She worked hard until she had qualified
herself to do the work.

她努力到有資格勝任這項工作。

衍生單字

☑ qualified *adj.* 合格的、有能力的、限制的
☑ qualification *n.* 資格、條件

track 132

assure

> v. 使確信、使放心、保證、擔保

例 句

🔘 I assure you that this medicine cannot harm you.

我向你保證這藥對你不會有害。

🔘 Visitors to our shop are assured of a gracious reception.

光臨本店的顧客保證受到禮貌接待。

衍生單字

☑ assurance *n.* 確信、斷言、保證、擔保

secure

> *adj.* 安全的、可靠的
> v. 得到、獲得、使安全、保衛、縛牢

同義 safe *adj.* 安全的

例 句

🔘 You have made me feel secure.

你使我感到安全。

🔘 Do you feel secure about your future?

你對未來感到放心嗎？

🔘 He secured the prisoner with ropes.

他用繩子把犯人綁牢。

track 133

guarantee

v. 保證、擔保

n. 保證、保證書

例 句

例 We can't guarantee our workers' regular employment.

我們無法保證工人們定期的雇用。

例 The watch is guaranteed for three years.

這支手錶保固三年。

例 We have a one-year guarantee on our new car.

我們買的新汽車保用一年。

同義 warrant v. n. 保證、擔保

imitate

v. 模仿、仿造、仿效

例 句

例 His handwriting is difficult to imitate.

他的筆跡很難模仿。

例 You should imitate his way of doing things.

你應當仿效他的做事方法。

衍生單字

☑ imitation n. 仿效、仿製品

☑ imitative *adj.* 仿造的
☑ imitator *n.* 仿造者、模仿者

let

| *v.* 讓、允許 |
| (*p. pp.*=let; let) |

例 句

例 Let's go.
我們走吧！

例 Let's go to see the movie.
我們去看電影吧！

例 Let me hold the door for you.
我幫你扶著門吧！

例 Let us go to help David, will you?
讓我們去幫助大衛好不好？

例 Let go of me.
放我走！

lie

| *v.* 躺臥、平放、位於 |
| (*p. pp. ppr.*=lay; lain; lying) |

例 句

例 You should lie down.
你應該躺下來。

例 I lay down on the grass. track 134
我躺在草地上。

track 134

例 The box is lying on the table.
這個盒子放在桌上。

find

v. 找到、發現、發現處於某種狀態
(*p. pp.*=found; found)

例 句

例 Did you find anything you like?
有找到你喜歡的了嗎？

例 I can't find my shoes.
我找不到我的鞋子。

lose

v. 丟失、迷路、輸、(鐘錶)走慢
(*p. pp.* =lost; lost)

例 句

例 A few books have been lost from the library.
圖書館遺失了幾本書。

例 She lost her way in the darkness.
她在黑暗中迷失了方向。

meet

v. 碰見、遇見、認識
(*p. pp.*=met; met)

track 134

例 句

例 I met David in the street yesterday.
昨天我在街上遇到大衛。

例 If you come, I'll meet you at the station.
如果你要來，我會到車站去接你。

例 How did you meet David?
你怎麼認識大衛的？

例 "Glad to meet you." "It's my pleasure."
「真高興認識你。」「我的榮幸。」

例 Have you ever met before?
你們以前見過面嗎？

session

n. 會議、一屆會期、集會

例 句

例 The session begins at six o'clock.
會議六點鐘開始。

例 This year's session of Congress was unusually long.
今年這屆國會的會期非常長。

 track 135

introduce

v. 介紹、傳入、引進、採用、提出

例　句

例 I'd like to introduce you to my friend, David.

大衛，我來介紹你給我的朋友認識。

例 He introduced a subject into the conversation.

他在談話中提出了一個話題。

衍生單字

☑ introduction *n.* 介紹、導論

follow

v. 跟隨、領會、沿著……前進、遵循、結果是…

例　句

例 The boy followed his father out.

這男孩跟著他父親出來。

例 Do you follow what I am saying?

我說的話你聽懂了嗎？

例 It follows that she must be innocent.

結果她肯定是無罪的。

feel

v. 觸摸、感覺、覺得、想要
(*p. pp.*=felt; felt)

例　句

例 The doctor felt my arm to find out if it was broken.

醫生摸摸我的手臂，看看是否斷了。

例 I feel awful.

我覺得糟透了。

例 Would you feel like a cup of coffee?

你要喝咖啡嗎？

fit

v.	使適合、使配合、適應、安裝
adj.	適合的、恰當的、健康的、強健的

例　句

例 Her special abilities fit her well for the job.

她的特殊才能使她很適合做這份工作。

例 Can you help me to fit this shelf to that wall?

你能不能幫我把這架子裝到那片牆上去？

例 He keeps himself fit by running 5 miles every day.

他每天跑五英里以保持身體健康。

track 136

sense

n.	官能、感覺、判斷力、見識、意義
v.	覺得、意識到

例 句

例 What you say makes no sense.

你說的話沒有道理。

例 She fully sensed the danger of her position.

她充分意識到她處境的危險。

perceive

v. 察覺、感知、認識到、意識到

例 句

例 I perceived a change in his behaviour.

我覺察出他的行為改變了。

例 I perceived that I could not make him change his mind.

我意識到我不能使他改變主意。

衍生單字

☑ perceivable *adj.* 可察覺的、可理解的

miss

v. 想念、思念、錯過、未擊中
n. 未中、達不到

例 句

例 I'll miss you.

我會想念你的。

例 He missed the bus.

他錯過了公車。

track 136

例 It's on the right side. You won't miss it.

就在右邊。你不會看不見的。

例 He hit the target three times without a miss.

他三發三中。

title

n. 頭銜、職稱、標題、書名

例 句

例 He was given the title of Marquis.

他被封為侯爵。

例 The title of the novel is "The Six".

該書的書名為《第六位》。

track 137

Miss

n. 小姐（對未婚女性的尊稱）

例 句

例 Miss Green is my English teacher.

格林小姐是我的英文老師。

例 Hey, Miss, you dropped a glove!

嘿，小姐，妳的手套掉了！

Mr.

n. （姓氏）先生、（職位的）尊稱

track 137

例 句

例 Good afternoon, Mr. Brown.

早安,布朗先生!

例 I'm afraid I can't agree with what's just been said, Mr. Chairman.

主席先生,我無法認同剛剛的言論。

• Mrs.

n. (姓氏)已婚夫人

例 句

例 Mrs. Smith lives in Paris.

史密斯太太住在巴黎。

例 Mr. and Mrs. Brown are married and live together in their own home

布朗夫婦已經結婚並一起住在他們自己的房子裡。

• boy

n. 男孩、少年、兒子
int. 哇(表示驚喜、訝異)

反義 **girl** *n.* 女孩

例 句

例 Don't cry. You're a big boy now.

別哭啦!你已是個大孩子囉!

track 137

例 We've got three children - a boy and two girls.

我們有三個孩子，一個男孩，兩個是女孩。

例 It's no problem, my boy.

沒問題啦，小老弟！

例 Boy! Isn't it cool!

哇！真是酷啊！

相關單字

☑ man *n.* 男(複數 men)
☑ woman *n.* 女(複數 women)
☑ male *n.* 男性
☑ female *n.* 女性
☑ gentleman *n.* 紳士
☑ madam *n.* 夫人

track 138
☑ boyfriend *n.* 男朋友
☑ girlfriend *n.* 女朋友
☑ soul mate *n.* 靈魂伴侶
☑ lover *n.* 戀人

marry

v. 結婚

例 句

例 Will you marry me?

和我結婚吧！（求婚）

例 He never married.

他沒有結過婚！

相關單字

☑ separate *v.* 分居

☑ divorce *v.* 離婚

marriage

n. 婚姻、婚禮

例 句

例 It was a very happy marriage.

那是一段很美滿的婚姻。

例 The marriage will take place next month.

婚禮將於下個月舉行。

相關單字

☑ bachelor party *n.* 告別單身漢派對

☑ wedding shower *n.* 告別單身女子派對

☑ couple *n.* 夫婦

☑ husband *n.* 丈夫

☑ wife *n.* 妻子

☑ widower *n.* 鰥夫

☑ widow *n.* 寡婦

☑ fiance *n.* 未婚夫

☑ fiancee *n.* 未婚妻

☑ groom *n.* 新郎

☑ bride *n.* 新娘

☑ best man *n.* 伴郎

☑ maid of honor *n.* 伴娘

☑ single *n.* 單身

program

n. 節目、方案、課程、程式

例　句

例 What is your favorite television program?

你最喜愛的電視節目是什麼？

例 The church offers religous programs for teens.

教堂為青少年安排了宗教活動。

 track 139

相關單字

- ☑ TV *n.* 電視
- ☑ channel *n.* 頻道
- ☑ cable channel *n.* 有線頻道
- ☑ drama *n.* 戲劇
- ☑ talk show *n.* 脫口秀
- ☑ soap opera *n.* 肥皂劇
- ☑ feature film *n.* 劇情片
- ☑ horror film *n.* 恐怖片
- ☑ war film *n.* 戰爭片
- ☑ comedy *n.* 喜劇片
- ☑ romance *n.* 浪漫片
- ☑ action film *n.* 動作片
- ☑ sci-fi film *n.* 科幻片
- ☑ western *n.* 西部片
- ☑ martial art *n.* 武俠片
- ☑ musical *n.* 音樂劇
- ☑ cartoon *n.* 卡通
- ☑ news *n.* 新聞
- ☑ documentary *n.* 紀錄片
- ☑ quiz show *n.* 智力競賽節目
- ☑ live broadcast *n.* 實況轉播
- ☑ TV advertisement *n.* 電視廣告
- ☑ weather forecast *n.* 天氣預報
- ☑ sports news *n.* 體育新聞

hope

v.	希望、期望
n.	希望、盼望、期望、被寄託希望的人或物

同義 wish v. n. 希望、盼望

例 句

例 I hope it'll be sunny tomorrow.
希望明天是個晴天。

例 "Maybe he'd call me." "I hope so."
「也許他會打電話給我。」「希望是這樣！」

例 He didn't give up his hope.
他並沒有放棄他的希望。

alarm

n.	警報、驚恐、驚慌
v.	告急、使警戒

同義 scare v. n. 驚恐、恐慌

例 句

例 I'm going to turn off the alarm.
我要去關掉設定警報。

例 The alarm was given for a fire.
火警警報發佈了。

例 We don't feel much alarm.
我們不會感到驚恐。

例 Don't be alarmed.
別慌！

track 140

call

v. n. 稱呼、打電話、呼喚、拜訪、命名

同義 shout *v.* 呼喊、大聲說

例 句

例 We'll call the baby Joan.

我們會給嬰兒取名瓊。

例 I'll call you at six.

我六點鐘會打電話給你。

例 Could I call on you on Monday?

我可以星期一去拜訪你嗎？

例 I made a long-distance call to New York.

我打了一通長途電話到紐約。

answer

v. n. 回答、答覆、接(電話)、應(門)、負責

例 句

例 Just answer me.

回答我就好！

例 I'll answer for the consequences.

我願為其後果負責。

例 What's your answer?

你的答案是什麼？

breath

n. 呼吸、氣息

例 句

例 When David walked out of the room, he drew a deep breath.

大衛走出房間,深深地吸了一口氣。

例 It has put me a little out of breath.

它使我有點喘不過氣。

announce

v. 宣佈、發表、通告、報告……的來到

例 句

例 The company has announced plans to open six new stores.

這家公司宣布要開六家新店的計畫。

例 He announced that he was going out.

他宣布他要出去。

例 Would you announce the guests as they come in?

客人來時你通報一聲好嗎?

衍生單字

☑ announcer *n.* 播音員、報幕員

track 141

declare

v. 宣佈、聲明、宣佈主張

例句

例 The Prime Minister declared his intention in the speech.

總理聲明演講的目的。

proclaim

v. 公佈、正式宣佈（政治、法律、方針、計劃等）

例句

例 We proclaimed these truths to be self-evident.

我們宣佈這些真理都是不證自明的。

publish

v. 公佈、發表、頒佈（法律、決議、發佈消息等）

例句

例 The rules and regulations will be published in the newspapers.

這些規章制度將在報紙上公佈。

buy

v. 購買

(*p. pp.*=bought; bought)

反義 sell *v.* 販售

例 句

⑩ I'll buy my wife a watch.

我要買一支錶給我的太太。

⑩ Did you buy her anything?

你有買任何東西給她嗎？

pay

n. 工資、薪水

v. 付錢、給報酬、給予注意、進行(訪問等)、值得

(*p. pp. ppr.*=paid; paid; paying)

類似 salary *n.* 薪水

wages *n.* 工資

例 句

⑩ How much should I pay?

我應該要付多少？

⑩ I'll pay you $30 to clean my garden.

我付你卅元去清洗我的庭院。

⑩ Pay attention to what I'm saying.

請注意我說的話。

track 142

例 It pays to choose good cloth for a suit.

選用好料子做一套衣服是值得的。

例 He gets his pay each Thursday.

他每星期四領工資。

衍生單字

☑ payment *n.* 支付、付款額

charge

v. n. 索價、要價、控告、充電

例 句

例 Her landlord charged her no rent.

她的房東不收她房租。

例 He was charged with murder.

他被控告犯謀殺罪。

例 The man in the garage said he would charge up my car battery.

修車廠的人說會把我的車子的蓄電池充電。

•enjoy

v. 喜歡、享有、欣賞

例 句

例 Did you enjoy yourself tonight?

你今晚玩得開心嗎？

例 I enjoyed the film.

我很喜歡這部電影。

track 142

例 I enjoyed the days in the USA.

我在美國過得很開心。

eat

v. 吃、食

(*p. pp.*=ate; eaten)

例 句

例 What would you like to eat?

你想吃什麼？

例 I can't eat anymore.

我吃不下了。

track 142

drink

v. 喝、飲、喝酒(*p. pp.*=drank; drunk)

n. 飲料、酒（常用複數表示）

例 句

例 What would you like to drink?

你想要喝什麼飲料？

例 Do you have any cold drinks?

你們有冷飲嗎？

track 143

drunk

adj. 酒醉的、陶醉的、著迷的

n. 酒鬼

track 143

例 句

例 He got drunk on only two drinks.

他只喝兩杯就醉了。

例 The man was dead drunk.

那人爛醉如泥。

例 She is drunk with joy.

她陶醉於歡樂之中。

need

v. n. 需要、必要

例 句

例 A friend in need is a friend indeed.

患難見真情。

例 Do you need help?

你需要幫助嗎？

例 You need to get some sleep.

你需要睡一下。

例 It'll need another 20 minutes.

還要再廿分鐘。

dry

v. 使…乾燥
adj. 乾燥的、乾旱的

例 句

例 I can't go out until my hair dries.

我得等頭髮變乾才能出門。

track 143

例 The paint is not yet dry.
油漆還沒有未乾。

例 It's getting dry.
快乾了。

bring

v. 帶來、拿來、帶領、引起、導致
(*p. pp.*=brought; brought)

例 句

例 Please bring me a napkin.
請幫我拿一條餐巾來。

例 I brought my daughter to the office.
我帶我女兒到辦公室。

例 This remark brought an outburst of laughter.
這句話引起了一陣笑聲。

track 144

carry

v. 提、扛、搬、運送、攜帶
(*p. pp. ppr.*=carried; carried; carrying)

類似 bring *v.* 攜帶

例 句

例 Can you carry the heavy box?
你搬得動這個重的盒子嗎？

track 144

例 I carried a basket in my hand.
我手裏拎著籃子。

例 Who is going to carry this box?
誰要拿這個盒子？

take

v.	拿、花費(時間)、吃喝(餐點、藥)、
	乘車(船)、帶領、奪取（性命等）
	(*p. pp.*=took; taken)

例 句

例 It may rain, so take your umbrella.
可能會下雨，所以你要帶著傘。

例 Take this medicine after each meal.
每頓餐後都要服用這個藥。

例 Please, take me with you!
拜託，帶我一起去。

例 The fire took her life.
火災奪走她的生命了！

brush

| n. | 刷子、毛刷、畫筆 |
| v. | 刷、擦、揮拂、擦過、掠過 |

例 句

例 You should brush your teeth every day.
你應該要每天刷牙。

例 She brushed her hair.
她每天梳頭髮。

track 144

例 I need a better brush for my hair.
我需要一把好一點的梳子來梳頭髮。

例 She brushed my arm with hers.
她用手臂輕撫我的手臂。

• borrow

v.	(向別人) 借、借用

反義　lend v. 出借

例 句

例 Could I borrow your bike until next week?
我能向你借腳踏車到下星期嗎？

例 May I borrow your magazines?
我可以向你借雜誌嗎？

例 I borrowed one hundred dollars from him.
我向他借了一百元。

 track 145

• lend

v.	出借
	(p. pp. = lent; lent)

例 句

例 Can you lend me a few dollars till payday?
你可以借我一些錢到發薪水那天嗎？

例 Who lent you the bike?

誰借給你這輛自行車？

begin

v.	開始、著手、創建、源於
	(*p. pp. ppr.*=began; begun; beginning)

例 句

例 He begins his new job on Monday.

他星期一開始新工作。

例 The movie begins at seven.

電影七點鐘開始。

例 I began by explaining why I had come.

我一開始就解釋為什麼我會來。

start

v. n. 開始、著手做、出發

反義	finish v. 完成

例 句

例 If everyone is ready, we can start.

如果每個人都準備好了，我們就可以開始了。

例 Shall we start?

我們可以開始了嗎？

例 That's a good start.

那是一個好的開始。

finish

| v. | 結束、做完 |

同義 complete v. 完成

例 句

例 I haven't finished reading that book yet.
我還沒有讀完那本書。

例 Have you finished reading that magazine?
你看完那本雜誌了嗎?

delay

| v. n. | 耽擱、延遲 |

 track 146

例 句

例 He wants to delay the meeting until Wednesday.
他想要把會議延遲到星期三。

例 Any further delay would threaten the entire project.
任何的延遲都會影響整個計畫。

postpone

| v. | 推遲、延期 |

同義 delay v. 推遲
suspend v. 延期

track 146

例 句

例 We are postponing our holiday until August.

我們把休假延到八月。

例 The party was postponed a few days.

派對延期了幾天。

衍生單字

☑ postponable *adj.* 可延緩的

☑ postponement *n.* 延遲、延期

深入分析

1. postpone 指因主觀原因而延期到一特定時間。

☞ They are postponing their trip until the weather grows warmer.

他們把旅行延期到天氣變暖的時候。

2. delay 強調延緩之概念，常指因某種客觀上原因而延緩，稍後可能再繼續做，但也指無限延期。

☞ Their arrival will be delayed because of heavy traffic.

因為交通堵塞，他們將延後抵達。

stop

v.	停止、阻止
	(*p. pp.*=stopped; stopped)
n.	停止、車站

例 句

例 You should stop smoking.

你應該要戒煙。

例 You must stop her from telling such lies.

你必須阻止她撒這種謊言。

例 I'm going to get off at the next stop.

我要在下一站下車。

become

v. 變得、成為

(*p. pp.*=became; become)

例 句

例 He became a US citizen last year.

他去年成為美國公民了。

 track 147

例 We became actual friends.

我們變成真正的朋友了。

ask

v. 詢問、請求

例 句

例 Can I ask you a question?

我可以問你一個問題嗎？

例 You should ask your lawyer for advice.

你應該要問問你的律師的意見。

例 I have other plans. Thanks for asking, though.

我有其他計畫了。還是感謝你的邀請。

例 "Are you going to David's party?" "No, I haven't been asked."

「你要去大衛的派對嗎？」「沒有，我沒有被邀請。」

demand

n.	要求、請求、需求(量)
v.	要求、請求、需求、查問

例 句

例 He demands that he be told everything.

他要求將一切都告訴他。

例 The policeman demanded the boys' names.

警察查問孩子們的名字。

• request

v.	請求、要求、懇求

例 句

例 We request the pleasure of your company for dinner.

敬請光臨參加宴會。

claim

v.	要求、聲稱、主張、索賠
n.	要求、主張、斷言、索賠、權利、所有權

同義	affirm	*v.* 宣稱
	request	*v.* 請求、要求

例 句

例 If no one claims the money, I can keep it.

如果沒有人認領這筆錢，我就可以擁有這些錢。

例 She claimed £500 from him for injuries suffered.

她向他索取500英鎊的賠償費。

例 Did you get the claim you asked for?

你得到要求的權利了嗎？

衍生單字

☑ claimant *n.* 請求者、主張者

 track 148

complain

v. 抱怨、申訴

同義	grumble	*v.* 發牢騷、喃喃抱怨
	murmur	*v.* 低聲抱怨

例 句

例 She complained that he did not work hard.

她抱怨他工作不努力。

例 She complained that she had too much work to do.

她抱怨工作太多。

例 He complained of ill treatment.

他申訴遭受虐待。

persuade

v. 説服、勸説、使相信

反義 dissuade *v.* 勸阻勿做…

例 句

例 She tried to persuade them that they should leave.

她試著説服他們應該要離開。

例 He persuaded me out of the idea of dropping the experiment.

他説服我打消中斷實驗的想法。

例 I am almost persuaded of his honesty.

我幾乎相信他是誠實的。

衍生單字

☑ persuasion *n.* 説服、説服力

count

v. 數、計算、算入、認為
n. 計數、計算、總數

例 句

例 He counted up to 10 and then came to find us.

他數到十，然後來找我們。

例 She was counted among the greatest dancers of the century.

她被認為是本世紀最偉大的舞蹈家之一。

track 148

例 I want you to start on a count of 5.

我數到五的時候，你就可以開始。

 track 149

rate

n. 速率、比率、等級、價格、費用

v. 估價、評級、評價

例 句

例 The birth rate is the number of births compared to the number of the people.

出生率是出生數與人口數的比較。

例 He did not rate the machine above its real value.

他沒有對這台機器估價過高。

control

n. v. 控制、支配

例 句

例 He has no control over his emotions.

他控制不住自己的感情。

例 The car went out of control and crashed.

汽車失去控制撞壞了。

例 It's hard to control your temper when you're two years old.

兩歲的人很難控制脾氣。

compromise

v. n. 妥協、折衷

例 句

例 They were refusing to compromise on it.
他們拒絕妥協。

例 I hope we shall come to a compromise.
希望我們能達成妥協。

例 Most wage claims are settled by compromise.
對提高工資的要求大多都能折衷解決。

describe

v. 形容、說明、敘述、描寫

例 句

例 The scientists described their findings and research methods.
科學家說明他們發現和研究的方法。

例 Just describe what happened.
只要說明發生什麼事就可以了！

mind

n. 心思、頭腦、想法、主意
v. 介意、在意、留意

track 150

例 句

例 We changed our minds about selling the house.

關於賣房子的事我們改變主意了！

例 I haven't made up my mind whether to go yet.

我還沒有決定要去哪裡！

例 I'll keep you in mind if another job comes up.

如果有其他工作，我會替你留意。

例 Do you mind not smoking in here, please?

可以請你不要在這裡抽菸嗎？

例 I don't mind.

我不在意！

例 Would you mind if I borrowed your book?

我可以借用你的書嗎？

• invest

v. 投資

例 句

例 He's invested a million dollars in the project.

他在這項計畫上投資一百萬元。

衍生單字

☑ investment n. 投資

keep

v.	保持、保存、保留
	(p. pp.=kept; kept)

例句

例 Keep the change.

不用找零錢了！

例 Keep in touch.

要保持聯絡喔！

例 You can keep it; I don't need it.

你可以將它留下，我不需要了。

contact

n. v. 接觸、聯繫

例句

例 We must keep in contact with the masses.

我們必須與群眾保持聯繫。

例 We'll contact John directly.   track 151

我們將直接與約翰聯繫。

例 I'll contact you by phone on Friday.

我會在星期五打電話和你聯繫。

connect

v. 連接、連結

例句

例 The printer connects to the computer.

這台印表機有連接到電腦。

例 Connect me with Hong Kong, please.

請給我接通香港。

• disguise

n. v. 假裝、偽裝

例 句

例 Nobody saw through his disguise.

誰都沒有看穿他的偽裝。

例 She disguised herself as a man.

她假扮成男人。

• cook

v.	烹調、烹煮
n.	廚師

例 句

例 Do you know how to cook onion soup?

你知道如何煮洋蔥湯嗎？

例 I'm going to cook dinner tomorrow.

明天我要做晚飯。

例 David is a good cook.

大衛是一位好廚師。

衍生單字

☑ cooker *n.* 烹飪用具

track 151

cut

v.	切、剪、割、削、縮減（預算等）
n.	刀傷、剪、割

例 句

例 Cut the apple in half.
把蘋果對半切開。

例 I cut my fingers on the broken glass.
我被破玻璃割破手指。

例 We've got to cut costs.
我們要縮減預算。

例 He had a cut on his face. track 152
他的臉上有一道刀傷。

shave

v.	剃(鬍鬚、毛髮等)、修短(樹叢、草地等)
n.	刮鬍鬚

例 句

例 He finally shaved his beard.
他最後還是剃了鬍子。

例 The barber gave him a shave and a haircut.
理髮師幫他修鬍子和理髮。

shape

n.	形狀、外形、情況、狀態、種類
v.	成形、塑造

track 152

例 句

例 All circles have the same shape.

所有圓的形狀都一樣。

例 He shaped the clay into a vase.

他將泥土塑成花瓶。

close

v.	關、閉
adj.	接近的、靠近的、親密的
adv.	靠近地

例 句

例 Don't forget to close the door.

不要忘記要關門。

例 The shop has been closed though it is only 3 pm.

儘管才下午三點鐘，商店已經關門了。

例 He followed close behind me.

他緊跟在我的後面。

例 Tracy is my closest friend.

崔西是我最親密的朋友。

open

| v. | 打開、張開 |
| adj. adv. | 開著的、開口的 |

反義 close v. 關上

例 句

例 I opened the window a minute ago.
我一分鐘之前才把窗戶打開的。

例 The window was wide open.
窗戶開得非常大。

衍生單字

☑ opening n. 口、孔、開始、空缺
           adj. 開始的、開幕的

track 153

play

v.	玩、打球、參與（活動等）、演奏樂器
n.	玩耍、戲劇

例 句

例 They are playing games.
他們正在玩遊戲。

例 What team does she play for?
她為哪一隊效力？

例 I like playing basketball.
我喜歡打籃球。

例 Do you know how to play guitar?
你知道怎麼彈吉他嗎？

例 We went to see the play yesterday.
我們昨天去看戲了。

clean

v.	弄乾淨、打掃
adj.	乾淨的、清潔的

track 153

例　句

例 Did you clean your room?

你有打掃房間嗎？

例 Please clean it up.

請清理乾淨。

例 The floor is clean.

地板很乾淨。

clear

| v. | 澄清、清除、收拾 |
| adj. | 清楚的、明朗的 |

例　句

例 It took several hours to clear the road after the accident.

事故發生後花了好幾個小時路面才清理乾淨。

例 Just let me clear the dishes off the table.

先讓我清理一下桌面。

例 It wasn't clear what he meant.

他表達的意思並不清楚。

pull

| v. | 拉、拖、拔(瓶塞、牙齒等)、牽 |
| n. | 拉、拖、拉力、把手 |

反義　push v. 推

例 句

 track 154

例 Can you pull it for me?

可以幫我拉一下嗎？

例 I couldn't pull the boat out of the water.

我無法把小船從水裡拉出來。

例 I had the bad tooth pulled out.

我把那顆蛀牙拔了。

push

| v. | 推、推進、逼迫 |
| n. | 推、擠、努力 |

例 句

例 You have to push the button.

你應該要按按鈕。

例 Please push the car!

請推一下這輛車！

例 I gave the window a push.

我推了那扇窗戶。

insert

| v. | 插入、嵌入 |

例 句

例 I wish to insert an advertisement in your newspaper.

我希望能在你們的報紙上登一則廣告。

例 Insert the key in the lock.

把鑰匙插進鎖孔中。

track 154

draw

v.	畫、繪製、拉、拖、牽
	(p. pp.=drew; drawn)

同義 pull *v.* 拉、拖

例 句

例 What did you draw?
你畫了什麼？

例 David draws very well.
大衛畫得很好。

例 He drew the chair toward David.
他把椅子拉向大衛。

衍生單字

☑ drawer *n.* 拖曳者、抽屜

lift

v.	升起、舉起
n.	升起、電梯、免費搭車

例 句

 track 155

例 I can't lift you up. You're a big boy now!
你現在長大了，我抱不動你。

例 Is the lift going up or down?
電梯在向上開還是向下開？

例 He offered me a lift.

他讓我免費搭車。

衍生單字

☑ lifter *n.* 起重機、舉重運動員

operate

v. 運轉、開動、動手術、開刀

例 句

例 This machine operates day and night.

這台機器日夜運轉。

例 You can get a private doctor to operate on him.

你可以找個私人醫生給他動手術。

衍生單字

☑ operation *n.* 運轉、開動、操作、算術

withdraw

v. 收回、撤消、縮回、退出、提取(錢)

(*p. pp.* = withdrew; withdrawn)

例 句

例 I don't want to to withdraw what I've just said.

我不想收回我剛才說的話。

例 They withdraw from the competition.

他們退出比賽。

track 155

例 He withdrew all his money from the bank.
他把所有的存款從銀行裡提了出來。

insist

| v. | 堅持、強調 |

例 句

例 They insisted on their original view.
他們仍堅持原來的觀點。

例 He insisted on driving her home.
他堅持開車送她回家。

例 He insisted that I should be present.
他堅持要讓我出席。

衍生單字

☑ insistence n.   堅持
☑ insistent adj.   堅持的、強求的

track 156

put

| v. | 放、擺、裝、施加、寫上、穿衣 |
| | (p. pp.= put; put) |

同義 place v. 放、擺

例 句

例 Remember to put your hat here.
記得要把你的帽子放在這裡。

例 Don't forget to put on your coat.
不要忘記穿上你的外套。

例 I put you down for the trip next week.
我把你列入下星期的旅遊名單中。

locate

| v. | 找地點、坐落於 |

例 句

例 Can you locate the hospital on the map?
你能在地圖上找到這家醫院的位置嗎？

例 The museum is located on Maple Street.
博物館位於楓葉街。

衍生單字

☑ location *n.* 地點

drop

n.	滴、落下、微量
v.	落下、下降、失落
	(*p. pp. ppr.* = dropped; dropped; dropping)

例 句

例 The water leaks from the tap drop by drop.
水一滴一滴地從水龍頭裏漏出來。

例 Will you have a drop of brandy?
你要喝點白蘭地嗎？

track 156

paste

v. 黏、貼

n. 糊、漿糊

例 句

例 You can stick paper with paste made of flour and water.

你可用麵粉和水做成的漿糊來黏紙。

例 She pasted posters onto the wall.

她把海報貼在牆上了。

migrate

v. 移居(國外)、遷移

例 句

track 157

例 When did Asians begin to migrate to the United States?

亞洲人何時開始向美國移民的？

immigrate

v. 移民進入

反義 emigrate v. 移居國外

track 157

例 句

例 His family immigrated to the United States in 1970.

他的家人在 1970 年移民來美國。

衍生單字

☑ immigrant *n.* 移入者
☑ emigrant *n.* 移出者

swing

v.	搖擺、搖蕩、回轉、旋轉
	(*p. pp.* = swung; swung)
n.	鞦韆、搖擺、擺動

例 句

例 The heavy door swung open.

這扇重門搖擺打開了！

例 The children are playing on the swings in the park.

孩子們正在公園裏盪鞦韆。

shake

n. v.	搖動、搖、顫抖、震動
	(*p. pp. ppr.* = shook; shaken; shaking)

例 句

例 We knew he'd get the shakes when he saw the enemy.

我們知道他看到敵人時會發抖的。

track 157

例 The wind shook some blossoms from the trees.

風將樹上的一些花搖落。

hide

v.	隱藏、躲藏、隱瞞
	(p. pp. ppr.=hid; hidden; hiding)

例 句

例 He hid the jewelry under a rock in a court-yard.

他把珠寶藏在院內的一塊石頭下面。

例 Don't hide your feelings; say what you think.

不要隱瞞你的感受，你想什麼就說什麼。

track 158

guide

n.	指南、領導
v.	帶路、引導

例 句

例 A guide will show you round the Palace.

導遊將陪你們參觀宮殿。

例 David guided him to the reception-room.

大衛將他帶領到接待室。

continue

v. 繼續

例 句

⑩ They continued hoping there would be additional survivors.

他們持續相信會有另外的生還者。

⑩ They continued to meet every week.

他們繼續每週見面。

⑩ "Don't worry about me,"she continued.

「不必擔心我。」她繼續說道。

roll

v. 滾動、搖擺、捲、繞
n. 捲狀物

例 句

⑩ The coin rolled off the table.

硬幣滾下桌子去了。

⑩ Buy me a roll of film.

幫我買一捲底片。

gap

n. 裂縫、峽谷、分歧

例 句

⑩ She has a gap between her front teeth.

她的門牙有個縫。

衍生單字
☑ generation gap *n.* 代溝

order

n.	順序、訂單、命令
v.	命令、點餐

例 句

例 Things were in terrible order.
情況一團糟。

例 He ordered her to go. track 159
他命令她走。

例 What would you like to order?
你想點什麼？

pathetic

adj.	可悲的、憐憫的

| 同義 | miserable *adj.* 痛苦的、不幸的 |

例 句

例 It was pathetic to watch her condition deteriorate day by day.
看著她的健康狀況日益惡化，真是可憐。

cover

v.	覆蓋、遮蔽、包括、涉及
n.	蓋子、套子、書的封面

例 句

例 She covered the child with a blanket.
她用毯子蓋住孩子。

例 My book has a dark blue cover.
我的書是深藍色的封面。

cancel

v. 取消、撤消、刪除

同義 abolish *v.* 取消、廢除
eliminate *v.* 消除

例 句

例 He cancelled his order for the goods.
他取消了貨物訂購單。

例 The game was cancelled.
比賽已被取消。

例 He cancelled some unnecessary words in the article.
他將文章中不必要的字刪去。

erase

v. 擦掉、刪去

例 句

例 You can erase pencil marks with a rubber.
你可以用橡皮擦去鉛筆字跡。

例 Please erase his name from the list.
請把他的名字從名單中刪去。

track 159

衍生單字
☑ eraser *n.* 橡皮擦

track 160

remove

v. 除去、搬遷、移動、遷走、撤職

例 句

例 The boy was removed from school.

這男孩被學校除名了。

例 They're going to remove into a new building.

他們準備搬進一棟新大樓。

衍生單字
☑ removal *n.* 除去、移動、搬遷

abandon

v. 丟棄、離棄、放棄

例 句

例 The captain abandoned his burning ship.

船長放棄了著火的船。

例 The car was found abandoned near the village.

那輛汽車被發現遺棄在村子附近。

maintain

v. 維持、贍養、維修、保養、堅持、主張

例 句

例 We maintained a speed of 40 miles an hour.

我們保持每小時 **40** 英里的速度。

例 They also help us to maintain the machinary.

他們還幫助我們維修機器。

例 He maintained that he was innocent.

他堅持自己是無罪的。

衍生單字

☑ maintenance *n.* 維持、保持、維修、保養

搭配　maintain law and order 維持治安

maintain one's family 養家

maintain friendly relationship 保持友好關係

collide

v. 碰撞、衝突、抵觸

例 句

例 In running around the corner, John collided with another boy.

約翰在跑著拐過角落時與另一個男孩相撞。

 track 161

例 The government collided with Parliament over its industrial plans.

政府在工業規劃上與議會發生衝突。

衍生單字

☑ collision *n.* 碰撞、衝突

commend

v. 表揚、稱讚、推薦

例 句

例 He commended them for their enthusiasm.

他稱讚他們的熱情。

例 I can commend this man's work to you.

我向你推薦這個人的工作。

represent

v. 作為…代表、象徵、表示、表現、描繪

例 句

例 He represented Taiwan in the conference.

他代表台灣參加了這個會議。

例 The dove represents peace.

鴿子象徵和平。

例 He was not what they had represented him to be.

他並不是他們所描繪的那樣子。

track 161

create

v.	創造、創作、引起、造成、建立

例 句

⑩ A novelist creates characters and a plot.

小說家塑造人物並設計情節。

⑩ The noise created a disturbance.

那響聲引起了一場騷亂。

衍生單字

- ☑ creature *n.* 生物、產物、創造物
- ☑ creation *n.* 創造、創作
- ☑ creative *adj.* 有創造性的、有創造力的

• achieve

v.	完成、實現、達到、得到

同義	accomplish *v.* 完成、實現
	attain *v.* 完成、達到

例 句

⑩ They hope to achieve their goal by peaceful means.

他們希望透過和平手段達到目的。

track 162

⑩ One after another they achieved independence.

他們一個接一個地取得了獨立。

衍生單字
- ☑ achievable *adj.* 可完成的、能獲得的
- ☑ achievement *n.* 完成、成就

attain

v. 達到、獲得、抵達、值得

例 句

例 We must try hard to attain this standard.
我們必須努力達到這個標準。

例 He attained the position of minister.
他得到了部長的職位。

area

n. 面積、地區、區域、範圍、領域

例 句

例 There have been many developments in the area of language teaching.
語言教學領域已有很多新的發展。

例 There aren't any big stores in this area.
這個地區沒有什麼大商店。

district

n. 行政區、區、管區

track 162

例 句

例 A person must vote in his or her own district.

一個人必須在自己所處的地區投票選舉。

region

n. （較大範圍的）區域

例 句

例 Few people live in the cold regions of the world.

世界上很少有人住在寒冷的地區。

build

v. 建築、造、建設

(*p. pp.*=built; built)

例 句

例 What did you build?

你蓋了什麼？

例 When was the house built?

這棟房子是什麼時候建造的？

衍生單字

☑ building *n.* 建築物 track 163

establish

v. 建立、創辦、設立、確立、證實

例 句

例 This is a newly established institute.

這是一個新建的機構。

例 We are now comfortably established in our new house.

我們現在已舒舒服服地在新居裡安頓下來了。

衍生單字

☑ establishment *n.* 建立、設立、機構

• construct

v. 建設、建造、構造、創立

例 句

例 It takes about two years to construct a large bridge.

修建一座大橋需要大約兩年的時間。

例 He constructed a theory on the new principles.

他根據新的原理創立了一門學説。

save

v. 挽救、節省、儲蓄

反義 waste *v.* 浪費

例 句

例 David saved Tracy from falling.

大衛救了崔西，沒有讓她掉下去。

track 163

例 It'll save me a lot of time.

它會幫我省很多時間。

例 You've saved me 10 dollars.

你替我省了10元。

rescue

n. v. 營救、援救

例 句

例 He was rescued from drowning.

他在溺水時被人救起。

衍生單字

☑ rescuer *n.* 營救者

深入分析

1. rescue 指從危險、災禍中迅速有效的援救、搶救，一般指救人，也指搶救東西不致毀壞。

 track 164

☞ We rescued the crew of that sinking ship.

我們營救了那艘沈船上的船員。

2. save 為普通用語，指使受害者(或物)擺脫危險或災禍，使其生存(或保存)下來。

survive

v. 倖存、從…中逃走、比…活得長

例 句

例 He didn't survive long after the accident.

事故後不久他就死了。

衍生單字

☑ survivor *n.* 倖存者

reserve

v. 保留、留待、預訂、訂
n. 儲備、後備人員、保留

例 句

例 They reserve the right to make further re-presentation.

他們保留進一步提意見的權利。

例 The old man keeps a large reserve of fire-wood for cold weather.

那老人儲備了大量木柴供冬天使用。

衍生單字

☑ reservation *n.* 保留、預訂
☑ reserved *adj.* 預定的、保存著的

thank

v. n. 感謝、謝謝

例 句

例 Thank you.

謝謝！

track 164

例 Thank you so much.
非常感謝你。

例 I received a letter of thanks.
我收到了一封感謝函。

welcome

v. n. adj. 歡迎

例 句

例 Welcome home.
歡迎回來！

例 Welcome to Taipei!
歡迎光臨台北！

例 "Thank you." "You are welcome."
「謝謝你。」「不客氣！」

 track 165

hospitality

n. 好客、殷勤、款待

例 句

例 The natives are noted for their hospitality.
當地人以殷勤好客而聞名。

例 He thanked the ladies for their hospitality.
他感謝女士們的款待。

receipt

n. 收據、收到、接到

例 句

⑩ Ask her to give you a receipt when you pay the bill.

付錢後，請她給你一張收據。

think

v. 想、思考、認為

(*p. pp.*=thought; thought)

例 句

⑩ What do you think about it?

你覺得呢？

⑩ I'll think about it.

我會考慮看看。

⑩ I have to think it over.

我應該好好想想！

imagine

v. 想像、設想、料想

例 句

⑩ She imagines that people don't like her.

她認為人們不喜歡她。

track 165

衍生單字

☑ imagination *n.* 想像、空想、想像力

expect

v. 盼望、認為

類似 hope *v.* 希望

例 句

例 He's expecting you.

他正在等你來。

例 What else do you expect?

不然你還期望什麼？

 track 166

intend

v. 計劃、打算、想要

同義 mean *n.* 打算

例 句

例 The gift was intended for you.

這個禮物是要送給你的。

例 This is intended for publication.

這是準備出版的。

衍生單字

☑ intention *n.* 意圖、意向、目的

mean

v. 表示…的意思、意味著、意欲、打算
adj. 自私的、吝嗇的、卑鄙的

| 同義 | selfish *adj.* 自私的、小氣的 |

| 反義 | generous *adj.* 大方的、慷慨的 |

例 句

例 I mean this is impossible.

我的意思是說這是不可能的。

例 I don't believe he means any harm.

我不相信他有意要造成傷害。

例 David is mean with money matters.

大衛很吝嗇。

consider

v. 認為、把…看作、考慮、細想、照顧

例 句

例 He was considered a genius.

他被看作是天才。

例 We must consider their suggestion carefully.

我們必須仔細考慮他們的建議。

衍生單字

☑ considering *prep.* 關於

☑ considerable *adj.* 相當的、可觀的

☑ considerate *adj.* 體貼的、周到的

track 166

purpose

n. 目的、意圖、用途、效果

同義	intention *n.* 意圖
	effect *n.* 效果

例 句

例 The regulation failed to achieve its purpose.

這一規定沒有達到目的。

例 Don't waste your money; put it to some good purpose.

不要浪費你的錢,要用在好的用途上。

track 167

face

v. 面向、面對
n. 臉部

例 句

例 You've got to face it.

你必須要正視這件事。。

例 I don't want to lose face.

我不想丟面子。

衍生單字

☑ forehead *n.* 額頭

☑ temple *n.* 太陽穴

- ☑ eyebrow *n.* 眉毛
- ☑ eye *n.* 眼睛
- ☑ eyehole *n.* 眼窩
- ☑ eyelid *n.* 眼皮
- ☑ eyelashes *n.* 睫毛
- ☑ ear *n.* 耳朵
- ☑ nose *n.* 鼻子
- ☑ cheek *n.* 臉頰
- ☑ mouth *n.* 嘴
- ☑ lip *n.* 嘴唇
- ☑ jaw *n.* 頸
- ☑ chin *n.* 下巴
- ☑ tooth *n.* 牙齒(複數 teeth)
- ☑ tongue *n.* 舌頭

body

n. 身體、肉體、主文、屍體

例 句

例 Police found the body in a field.
警察在野外發現了屍體。

衍生單字

- ☑ head *n.* 頭部
- ☑ brain *n.* 腦部
- ☑ hair *n.* 頭髮
- ☑ neck *n.* 脖子
- ☑ chest *n.* 胸部
- ☑ abdomen *n.* 腹部
- ☑ shoulder *n.* 肩膀
- ☑ back *n.* 背部
- ☑ waist *n.* 腰部
- ☑ hip *n.* 臀部

- ☑ arm *n.* 手臂
- ☑ elbow *n.* 肘部
- ☑ hand *n.* 手
- ☑ palm *n.* 手掌
- ☑ fist *n.* 拳頭
- ☑ finger *n.* 手指
- ☑ back *n.* 手背
- ☑ wrist *n.* 手腕
- ☑ leg *n.* 腿
- ☑ knee *n.* 膝蓋
- ☑ ankle *n.* 踝
- ☑ foot *n.* 腳(複數 feet)
- ☑ toe *n.* 腳趾頭
- ☑ muscle *n.* 肌肉 track 168
- ☑ bone *n.* 骨頭

catch

v.	抓住、接住、捕獲、趕上(車輛)、患病
	(*p. pp.*= caught; caught)

例 句

例 I'm going to catch the train.

我要去趕搭火車。

例 You walk on and I'll catch up with you later.

你往前走,我稍後就會趕上你的。

例 You'll catch a cold if you don't put a coat on.

如果你不穿上外套就會感冒。

例 Catch you later.

再見囉!

track 168

try

v. 嘗試、努力、試驗

(*p. pp. ppr.*=tried; tried; trying)

例 句

例 I've tried it, but it didn't help.

我試過了。但是一點幫助都沒有。

例 I'll try my best.

我會盡力的。

attempt

n. v. 企圖、試圖

同義 try *v.* 嘗試

例 句

例 He attempted to lie.

他企圖說謊。

例 He attempted escaping.

他企圖逃跑。

例 He succeeded at his first attempt.

他第一次嘗試就成功了。

turn

v. 旋轉、轉動、轉變

例 句

track 168

例 Why are you turning here?

為什麼你要在這裡轉彎？

例 Please turn to page 10.

請翻到第十頁。

例 He turned on the radio.

他打開收音機。

例 Would you turn off the light?　　track 169

你可以關燈嗎？

switch

n.	開關、電閘、轉換、枝條、鞭子
v.	轉換、關閉、接通

例 句

例 We had to make a switch in our arrangements.

我們不得不把安排做一下調整。

例 He switched the boys with a birch switch.

他用樺樹條鞭打孩子。

例 Don't switch the TV off.

不要關掉電視機。

shift

v.	移動、轉移、改變、轉變
n.	轉換、轉變、班次

同義	transfer *v.* 轉移、轉變

例 句

例 Please help me to shift the book shelf about.

請幫我把書架挪動一下。

例 The wind has shifted to the southeast.

風向轉向東南方。

avoid

v. 避免

例 句

例 Try to avoid danger.

儘量避免危險。

例 You should try to avoid catching a cold.

你應儘量避免感冒。

例 The man tried to avoid answering her.

那個人儘量避免回答她。

深入分析

avoid 後接名詞或動名詞，不接不定式；avoid 表示避免成功，如果表示企圖避免而未成功，只能用 try to avoid。

escape

n. v. 逃避、逃漏、逃脫

例 句

例 She escaped being killed in the blast because she had not gone to work.

由於沒有去上班，她避免了在那次爆炸中遇難。

track 170

use

v. 使用、應用、慣常

例 句

例 How would you use it?

你會怎麼使用？

例 We use a computer to do all its accounts.

我們用電腦來計算所有帳目。

例 I used to live in Taipei.

我過去一向住在台北。

available

adj. 有空的、可利用的、可得到的

例 句

例 If I am not available, please contact my secretary.

如果我不在，請和我的秘書聯絡。

例 These data are readily available.

這些資料易於得到。

例 This is the only reference book available here.

這是這裡能得到的惟一的一本參考書。

visit

v. n. 參觀、訪問、拜訪

例　句

例 Can I visit you this weekend?

我這個週末可以去拜訪你嗎？

例 I always visit my parents every two months.

我每隔二個月拜訪我的雙親一次。

例 I hope to visit Japan this year.

我希望今年能到日本訪問。

wait

v. 等候、等待

例　句

例 "May I speak to David?" "Wait a moment, please."

「我可以和大衛說話嗎？」「請稍等！」

例 What are you waiting for?

你在等什麼？

例 Do you mind waiting a few minutes?

介意稍等片刻嗎？

衍生單字

☑ waiter *n.* 男侍者

☑ waitress *n.* 女侍者

track 171

await

v. 等待

例句

例 We have awaited your coming for days.

我們等待你的到來已有多天了。

例 There are no jobs awaiting those farmers.

那些農夫沒有工作可做。

深入分析

await為書面用語，比wait正式，後接名詞、動名詞，不接不定式 to。

dress

v. 穿衣、穿著
n. 服裝、女服、童裝

例句

例 I'll be ready in a moment; I'm dressing.

我一會兒就好，我正在穿衣服。

例 Try on this dress, please.

請試穿這件衣服。

例 You have to wear on evening an dress for the party.

你應該要穿晚禮服去參加派對。

track 171

drive

v.	駕駛、駕車、驅趕、迫使

(p. pp.=drove; driven)*

例句

例 Let me drive you home.
我開車送你回家吧！

例 It began to drive me crazy.
事情開始讓我發瘋了。

license

v.	准許、許可、認可
n.	執照、許可證、許可

例句

例 The policeman asked to see his driving license.
警察要求看他的駕照。

例 His license was suspended for six months.
他的執照被吊銷六個月了。

brake

n.	閘、制動器、煞車
v.	煞車、用閘使(車)放慢速度

例句

track 172

例 The brake didn't work.
煞車不靈了。

例 The car braked to a stop.
車被煞住了。

break

v.	割、打破、違反、摔斷、打碎
	(*p. pp.*=broke; broken)

例 句

例 I broke a glass in the kitchen.
我在廚房裡打破了一個玻璃杯。

例 It breaks my heart to see him so unhappy.
看見他這麼不快樂讓我很傷心。

例 He didn't know he was breaking the law.
他並不知道自己犯法了！

walk

v.	走過、沿…走、遛狗
n.	步行、走、散步

例 句

例 I like walking.
我喜歡散步。

例 Would you walk my dog, please?
可以請你遛我的狗嗎？

例 It's just a ten minutes' walk.
走路只要十分鐘。

track 172

stand

v.	站、站起、忍受
	(*p. pp.*=stood; stood)

例 句

例 Stand up, please.
請站起來。

例 I just can't stand him.
我就是受不了他！

sit

v.	坐、位於
	(*p. pp. ppr.*=sat; sat; sitting)

例 句

例 "Can I talk to you now?" "Sure. Sit down."
「我現在能和你說話嗎？」「當然可以。坐下吧！」

例 May I sit down here?
我能坐在這裡嗎？

例 He sat at his desk working.　　track 173
他坐在書桌前工作。

seat

n.	座位、席位

例 句

track 173

例 Excuse me, is this seat taken?

請問這個座位有人坐嗎?

例 Have a seat, please.

請坐!

sleep

v.	睡覺、與…上床(發生性關係)
	(p. pp.=slept; slept)
n.	睡眠、睡眠時間

例 句

例 Did you sleep with her?

你有和她發生關係嗎?

例 Do you want to get some sleep?

你想要睡一下嗎?

例 I haven't had enough sleep.

我睡眠不足。

run

v.	奔跑、行駛、競選、逃跑
	(p. pp. ppr.=ran; run; running)
n.	跑、奔跑

例 句

例 He runs five miles a day.

他一天跑五公里。

例 Will he run for Governor?

他會競選州長嗎?

track 173

例 I ran into an old friend in a pub.
我在酒吧碰到了一位老朋友。

例 I've got to run some errands.
我要去辦一些事。

dance

v. 跳舞

例 句

例 I haven't danced for a long time.
我很久沒有跳舞了。

例 What are your favorite dance steps?
你最喜愛的舞步是什麼？

衍生單字

☑ dancing *n.* 跳舞

track 174

相關單字

☑ waltz *n.* 華爾滋
☑ tango *n.* 探戈
☑ ballet *n.* 芭蕾舞
☑ yoga *n.* 瑜珈
☑ aerobics *n.* 有氧舞蹈
☑ belly dance *n.* 肚皮舞
☑ pilates *n.* 皮拉提斯
☑ jazz *n.* 爵士舞
☑ hip hop *n.* 嘻哈
☑ salsa *n.* 莎莎
☑ samba *n.* 森巴

- ☑ rumba *n.* 倫巴
- ☑ paso doble *n.* 鬥牛
- ☑ cha cha *n.* 恰恰
- ☑ jitterbug *n.* 吉魯巴
- ☑ tap dance *n.* 踢踏舞
- ☑ foxtrot *n.* 狐步

jump

v. n. 跳、跳躍

例 句

🔞 Can you jump this fence?

你能跳過籬笆嗎？

🔞 Who jumped the highest?

誰跳得最高？

🔞 Can you jump across this stream?

你能跳得過這條河川嗎？

slip

v. 滑倒、滑落、溜走
  (p. pp. = slipped; slipped)
n. 疏忽、小錯、口誤、筆誤

例 句

🔞 She slipped and fell on the ice.

她在冰上滑倒了。

🔞 She slipped away without being seen.

她悄悄溜走，沒人看見。

track 174

例 There were a few trivial slips in the translations.
譯文有幾處小錯誤。

• flight

| *n.* | 飛行、航班、班機、樓梯的一段 |

例 句

例 He took the 5 o'clock flight to Boston.
他搭乘五點鐘的班機去波士頓。

例 My bedroom is two flights up.
向上兩段樓梯便是我的臥室。

parade

| *n.* | 遊行、檢閱 |
| *v.* | 使列隊前進、遊行 |

同義 march *v.* 進行

例 句

例 The soldiers are on parade.　　track 175
士兵們在列隊接受檢閱。

例 They paraded down the street.
他們在馬路上遊行。

transport

| *v.* | 運輸、運送、搬運 |
| *n.* | 運輸、運送、運輸系統 |

track 175

例 句

例 Wheat is transported from the farms to mills.

小麥從農場運往麵粉廠。

例 Some of the goods were damaged in transport.

有些貨物在運輸過程中受到損壞。

例 I'd like to go to the concert, but I have no transport.

我很想去聽音樂會,但我沒有交通工具。

transfer

v. 轉移、調動、轉車、轉業、轉讓
(*p. pp.* = transferred; transferred)

例 句

例 The head office has been transferred from New York to London.

總部已由紐約移至倫敦。

例 He transferred to a new school.

他轉學到了一所新學校。

例 He transferred the shares to his son.

他把股份轉讓給了他的兒子。

encounter

n. v. 遇到、遭遇

track 175

例 句

例 Our encounter with the President at the airport was exciting.

我們在機場和總統不期而遇，真令人興奮。

例 I encountered many difficulties when I first started this job.

我開始做這項工作時，遇到許多困難。

commerce

n. 商業、貿易

例 句

 track 176

例 They are pushing their commerce into all parts of the globe.

他們正向全球各地擴展貿易。

例 He is engaged in commerce.

他從事商業。

衍生單字

☑ commercial *adj.* 商業上的

company

n. 公司、商號、同伴

例 句

track 176

⑩ This company pays well.

這家公司付的薪資很高。

⑩ He works in an export and import company.

他在一家進出口公司工作。

⑩ I will keep you company.

我將和你作伴。

⑩ I shall be glad of your company on the journey.

我會很高興可以在旅行中和你同行。

衍生單字

- ☑ president *n.* 董事長
- ☑ general manager *n.* 總經理
- ☑ supervisor *n.* 主管
- ☑ secretary *n.* 秘書
- ☑ personnel manager *n.* 人事經理
- ☑ engineer *n.* 工程師
- ☑ accounting *n.* 會計員
- ☑ business manager *n.* 業務經理
- ☑ merchandiser *n.* 商品業務員
- ☑ assistant *n.* 助理

enterprise

n. 企業、公司、事業

例 句

⑩ This enterprise is doing a good business.

這家企業生意興隆。

衍生單字

☑ enterpriser *n.* 企業家

job

n. 工作、職業、分內事

例 句

例 He got a job as a waiter.
他找到當侍者的工作了！

例 I'm looking for a job.
我正在找工作！

例 Good job.
幹得好！

 track 177

例 It's my job to water the plants.
澆花是我分內的事。

衍生單字

☑ job hunter *n.* 求職者
☑ job opening *n.* 徵才

occupation

n. 工作、職業

例 句

例 You need to put your name, address, and occupation on the form.
你要在表格內填上你的姓名、地址和職業。

track 177

position

n. 位置、身份、地位、立場、職位

例 句

例 The chair used to be in this position.

椅子原來是放在這兒的。

例 What's your position on this problem?

你對這個問題持什麼態度？

例 He applied for a senior position with the company.

他申請應徵這家公司的資深職務。

capitalist

n. 資本家、資本主義

例 句

例 Mr. Smith is a capitalist.

史密斯先生是資本家。

相關單字

- ☑ economist *n.* 經濟學家
- ☑ chemist *n.* 化學家
- ☑ physicist *n.* 物理學家
- ☑ biologist *n.* 生物學家
- ☑ scientist *n.* 科學家
- ☑ mathematician *n.* 數學家
- ☑ statistician *n.* 統計學家
- ☑ philosopher *n.* 哲學家
- ☑ politician *n.* 政治家

track 177

- ☑ linguist *n.* 語言學家
- ☑ botanist *n.* 植物學家
- ☑ archaeologist *n.* 考古學家
- ☑ geologist *n.* 地質學家
- ☑ volcanist *n.* 火山學家
- ☑ zoologist *n.* 動物學家
- ☑ physiologist *n.* 生理學家
- ☑ artist *n.* 藝術家
- ☑ playwright *n.* 劇作家　　 track 178
- ☑ composer *n.* 作曲家
- ☑ designer *n.* 設計家
- ☑ sculptor *n.* 雕刻家
- ☑ architect *n.* 建築師
- ☑ designer *n.* 服裝設計師
- ☑ model *n.* 模特兒
- ☑ poet *n.* 詩人

track 178

import

v. n. 進口

| 反義 | export *v. n.* 出口 |

例 句

例 We import a lot of cars from the USA.
我們從美國大量進口汽車。

相關單字

- ☑ item *n.* 項目
- ☑ purchase *v. n.* 購買
- ☑ sale *v. n.* 銷售
- ☑ budget *v. n.* 預算

- ☑ orders *n.* 訂單
- ☑ competition *n.* 競爭
- ☑ consumption *n.* 消費
- ☑ demand *v. n.* 需求
- ☑ outlet *n.* 銷路
- ☑ offer *n.* 報價
- ☑ monopoly *n.* 壟斷
- ☑ turnover *n.* 交易額
- ☑ deficit *n.* 赤字
- ☑ foreign trade deficit *n.* 外貿逆差
- ☑ foreign trade surplus *n.* 外貿順差

custom

n. 習慣、風俗、慣例、海關、關稅

例 句

例 A lot of the old customs are dying out now.
許多舊的習俗正在消失。

例 When visiting a foreign country, we must respect the country's customs.
去外國訪問時，必須尊重該國的風俗。

例 The customs were paid.
關稅已付。

深入分析

1. custom 用於某個社會或民族表示某長期形成的習俗，常常譯作「風俗」或「風俗習慣」。

☞ The celebration of Christmas is a custom.
慶祝耶誕節是一種習俗。

2. habit 主要用於個人，表示其自覺形成的(好的或不好的)傾向性行為，一般譯作習慣。

track 178

☞ I got into the habit of drinking coffee every morning.

我習慣每天早上喝咖啡。

track 179

customer

n. 顧客、主顧

例　句

例 I have to pick up one of my customers.

我得要去接我的一位客戶。

contract

n. 合同、契約
v. 訂合同、訂契約、收縮

同義	shrink *v.* 縮小、收縮
	compress *v.* 壓縮、濃縮

例　句

例 We have entered into a contract with him.

我們已和他訂了契約。

例 They have been contracted to build a new bridge.

他們已立約承建那座新橋。

衍生單字

☑ contractor *n.* 承造者、承包商

track 179

stock

n. 備料、庫存、現貨、股票、公債
v. 儲備

例 句

例 This store keeps a large stock of shoes.
那家商店有許多庫存鞋子。

例 They've stocked their crops in the barn.
他們已把糧食儲存到糧倉裡了。

interview

n. 面試、會見
v. 接見、會見、面談、面試、採訪

例 句

例 I have an interview with him.
我和他有約。

例 I wanted to interview him about his research work.
我想採訪有關他研究工作的情況。

衍生單字

☑ interviewer *n.* 接見者、主試人
☑ interviewee *n.* 被接見者、被面試者

track 180

credit

n.	信譽、榮譽、稱讚、信用貸款、學分
v.	記入貸方、信任

例 句

例 Do you give credit to what the newspaper reported?

你相信那份報紙的報導嗎？

例 He deserves credit for his devotedness to the people's cause.

他獻身人民的事業精神值得讚揚。

例 The bank granted him a $5,000 credit.

銀行向他提供 5000 美元的貸款。

例 It takes 124 credits to graduate.

畢業須修滿 124 個學分。

例 Please credit it to my account.

請把這筆帳記到我帳上。

例 He could not credit her explanation.

他不能相信她的解釋。

衍生單字

☑ creditor n. 債權者

☑ creditable adj. 很好的

相關 credit card 信用卡

chief

n.	首領、領袖
adj.	主要的、首要的

同義	principal *adj.* 主要的、重要的
	main *adj.* 主要的

例 句

例 The president is the chief of the armed forces.

總統是武裝部隊的領袖。

例 He is the chief of the tribe.

他是這個部落的酋長。

例 His chief problem was getting a job.

他的首要問題是找工作。

例 He is the chief executive of the department.

他是該部門的主管。

crew

n.	全體船員、(機務人員)一組工作人員

例 句

例 The entire crew was killed in the plane crash.

在飛機失事中全體工作人員遇難。

例 The crew was large.

track 181

機組人員有很多。

track 181

例 The crew were all excited.

機組人員都很激動。

staff

| *n.* | 全體職員、參謀部 |
| *v.* | 為⋯配備人員 |

例 句

例 The manager was going to cut down the office staff.

經理將裁減辦公室工作人員。

例 All the staff are off today.

全體人員今天休假。

average

n.	平均數、平均
adj.	平均的、平常的、一般的
v.	平均

例 句

例 Their language development is below average.

他們的語言發展低於平均水準。

probability

| *n.* | 概率、可能性、或然性 |

例 句

track 181

例 He must calculate the probability of failure.

他必須計算一下失敗的機率。

例 There's little probability of reaching London tonight.

今晚幾乎不可能到達倫敦了。

衍生單字

☑ probable *adj.* 很可能的、大概的

☑ probably *adv.* 大概、或許、很可能

about

adv. 到處、大約

prep. 關於、在各處

例 句

例 "How are you doing?" "Great. How about you?"

「你好嗎？」「不錯！你呢？」

例 It took me about five minutes to get there.

我大約花了五分鐘的時間才到那裡。

例 How about going for a walk?　　track 182

要不要去散散步？

with

prep. 帶有、具有、用…、跟…一起

例 句

例 That book with a green cover is mine.

那本綠封面的書是我的。

例 What will you buy with the money?

你想用這些錢買什麼？

例 She is staying with a friend.

她正和一個朋友在一起。

beside

prep. 除…之外(還)

例 句

例 Come and sit here beside me.

過來坐在我旁邊。

例 That's beside the point.

那事與此不相干。

at

prep. 〔表示地點、位置〕在…(裡、上、旁等)、〔表示時間〕在…時間、〔表示動作的目標和方向〕朝向…、〔表示年齡〕在…、〔動作的出發點〕向…、對…

例 句

例 He stood at the door.

他站在門口。

例 I often get up at 6 o'clock.

我經常在六點鐘起床。

track 182

例 He shot at the bird, but missed it.

他瞄準小鳥射擊，但沒射中。

例 I often stay at home on Sunday.

星期天我經常待在家裡。

例 Don't laugh at me.

別嘲笑我！

衍生單字

- ☑ at first   起先
- ☑ at home   在家 (裡)
- ☑ at last   最後、終於
- ☑ at the moment   此刻
- ☑ at once   立刻、馬上
- ☑ at the same time   同時
- ☑ at the top of   在…頂部
- ☑ be good at   擅長

track 183

by

prep. 在…旁邊、〔時間〕不遲於、被 (表被動語態的動作主語)、用、由 (方法、手段)、乘 (交通工具等)

例 句

例 Sit by me.

在我旁邊坐下。

例 Be there by four o'clock.

四點鐘之前要到那裡。

例 He was struck by thunder.

他遭雷擊了。

track 183

例 I like to travel by train.

我喜歡坐火車去旅行。

例 By good luck I succeeded.

很幸運的，我成功了。

衍生片語

☑ by bus   乘公共汽車
☑ by train   坐火車
☑ by air (=by plane) 坐飛機
☑ by sea (=by ship)   坐輪船
☑ by bike   騎自行車
☑ by the way   順便
☑ day by day   天天、日復一日

because

conj. 因為、因……、由於〔某種因素〕

例 句

例 I got angry because he was late.

因為他遲到了，所以我很生氣。

例 Because it was raining heavily, I went back.

因為那時天正下著大雨，所以我就回去了。

after

adv. 後來、以後
conj. 在…以後

track 183

| 反義 | before *adv. conj.* 之前 |

例 句

例 What did you do after school?

放學後你做了什麼事？

例 She is not very strong after her illness.

她病後身體不太好。

before

adv. 以前
conj. 在…之前

例 句

 track 184

例 Have you ever been to Japan before?

你以前有去過日本嗎？

例 Have you two met each other before?

你們兩人以前見過面嗎？

例 I've never seen the movie before.

我以前從沒看過這部電影。

例 Before you came home, we already
cleaned the house.

在你回家之前，我們就已經打掃好房子了！

• ago

adv. 以前、(自今)…前

例　句

例 My grandfather died many years ago.

我爺爺好多年前就過世了！

例 He left five minutes ago.

他五分鐘前就離開了。

例 It's been many years ago.

已經是好多年前的事了！

• already

adv. 已經、早已

例　句

例 "Are you going to join me?" "I'd love to.
But I've already got plans."

「你要加入嗎？」「我是很想。但是我已經有計畫了。」

例 I've seen the movie already.

我已經看過這部電影了。

例 He already finished it.

他已經完成了！

away

adv. 不在、離…之遠

反義　near *adv.* 近的

例　句

track 184

例 "Has David come back yet?" "No, he's still away."

「大衛回來了嗎？」「沒有，他還沒回來！」

例 He's away from home.

他不在家。

例 His office is only three blocks away.

他的辦公室距離這裡只有三個街區遠。

衍生片語

☑ go away　走開
☑ be away　缺席、離開
☑ take away　拿開
☑ throw away　扔掉

track 185

back

adv.	向後、回原處
adj.	背面的、反面的
n.	背後、後面

例 句

例 Don't look back.

不要向後看。

例 Please ask her to call me back.

請她回我電話！

例 I'll be right back in a minute.

我馬上就回來。

例 David patted me on the back.

大衛在我背上輕拍了一下。

down

adv. 向下、往下、倒下
prep. 沿著(街道、河流) 向下

| 反義 | up *adv. conj.* 往上 |

例 句

例 Come on, you have to lie down.
　　來吧，你得要躺下來。

例 There's a bank down the corridor.
　　有一間銀行在走廊的最後。

例 You may keep walking down the street.
　　你可以沿這條街繼續往下走。

up

adv. 向上、在上、起立、起來、完了、終結

例 句

例 Stand up when the teacher comes in!
　　老師進來時要起立!

例 He drank up the milk.
　　他把牛奶全喝光了。

衍生片語

☑ up and down　　上上下下、來回地
☑ look up　　　　抬頭看
☑ put up　　　　舉起來
☑ sit up　　　　坐起來

track 185

here

adv.	這裡、向這裡、這時
n.	這裡

反義	there adv. n. 那裡

 track 186

例 句

例 Hi, I'm here to meet Mr. Smith.

嗨，我來見史密斯先生。

例 I'll tell Mr. Smith you are here.

我會告訴史密斯先生您來了。

例 Here comes my bus.

我的公車來了。

例 It's pretty far from here.

離這裡很遠！

there

adv.	在那裡、往那裡、在那個方面、你看、有 (與 be 動詞連用)
n.	那裡

例 句

例 It's over there.

在那邊。

例 Can I get there by bus?

我可以搭乘公車到那裡嗎？

例 There is nothing on your business!

不關你的事！

just

adv. 正好、剛才、僅僅

例 句

例 Hi, honey, just wondering what you are doing.

嗨，親愛的，我在想你正在做什麼？

例 Look, it's just in front of you.

看，就在妳面前。

例 "I worry about you." "Just relax."

「我真的很擔心你。」「放輕鬆！」

maybe

adv. 大概、也許(表示可能性)

例 句

例 Maybe you can ask the police officer.

也許你可以問警察。

例 "Will you come tonight?" "Maybe."

「你今晚會來嗎？」「也許會吧！」

never

adv. 決不、從來沒有

例　句

例 I've never met such a strange man.

我從沒碰到過這麼奇怪的人。

 track 187

例 "Have you ever been to Hong Kong?" "Never."

「你去過香港嗎？」「從沒有去過！」

例 You may never know the truth about what happened.

你可能永遠不知道發生事情的真相。

yes

adv. 是、好、同意

反義	no *adv.* 不、沒有

例　句

例 "Do you like dogs?" "Yes, I do."

「你不喜歡狗嗎？」「是的，我喜歡。」

例 "Are you ready?" "Yes, I am."

「你準備好了嗎？」「是的，準備好了。」

衍生單字

☑ yesman *n.* 應聲蟲

not

adv. 不、沒…

track 187

例 句

例 "Would you like to have dinner with me?"
"Sure, why not?"

「想要和我一起吃晚餐嗎？」「當然好，為什麼
不要呢？」

例 I'm sorry, but he is not at his desk.

很抱歉，但是他不在他的座位上。

now

adv. 現在、此刻

例 句

例 Do you have any idea where he is now?

你知道他現在在哪裡嗎？

例 Are you busy now?

你現在忙嗎？

例 I'll do it right now.

我現在馬上去做。

often

adv. 經常地、通常地

例 句

例 I often go to school on foot.

我經常走路去上學。

track 188

例 David often comes in the afternoon.
大衛下午常來。

例 How often do you go there?
你隔多久去那裡一次？

• usually

adv. 通常地、經常地

| 反義 | unusually *adv.* 不經常地 |

例 句

例 We usually go shopping.
我們經常去購物。

例 I usually take a walk after supper.
我通常在晚飯後散步。

例 David usually gets up early.
大衛經常很早就起床。

always

adv. 總是、一直、永遠、始終

例 句

例 I always walk my dog in the morning.
我總是在早上遛狗。

例 I always visit Mr. Jones every two months.
我每隔二個月拜訪瓊斯先生一次。

例 David always walks me home.

大衛總是會陪我走路回家。

• sometimes

adv. 有時地、不時地

例 句

例 Sometimes we go to see a movie.

有的時候我們會去看電影。

例 "Do you think we're close?" "Sometimes. Why?"

「你認為我們親密嗎？」「有的時候是啊！為什麼要這麼問？」

finally

adv. 最後地、最終地

同義 eventually *adv.* 最後地、最終地

例 句

例 He finally found his key.

最後他終於找到他的鑰匙了。

例 What decision did you finally make?

你們最後做出了什麼決定？

例 "I decided to give it up." "Finally."

「我決定要放棄了！」「你終於這麼做了！」

track 189

really

adv. 真正地、確實地

例 句

例 We really need your help.
我們真的需要你的幫忙。

例 "I've found a job." "Really?"
「我找到工作了。」「真的嗎？」

例 I really don't want it anymore.
我真的不想再要了。

例 "Do you want to have a dog?" "Not really."
「你想養狗嗎？」「不盡然希望！」

too

adv. 也、太

例 句

例 I can speak French, too.
我也會説法語。

例 "Nice to meet you!" "Nice to meet you, too."
「真高興認識你。」「我也很認識你。」

例 It's too cold to go swimming.
天氣太冷，不能去游泳。

very

adv. 很、非常

例　句

例 I like you very much.

我非常喜歡你。

例 "Let me help you with it." "Thanks. That is very kind of you."

「我來幫你忙。」「謝謝！你真好。」

例 It's not very far from here.

離這裡不會很遠。

even

adv.	甚至、連…都
adj.	均勻的、平坦的、雙數的
v.	使相等

反義　odd *adj.* 奇數的

例　句

例 He even doubts the facts.

他甚至懷疑事實。

例 The country is even, with no high mountains.

這個國家地勢平坦，無高山。

例 The two boxers were even in strength.

這兩個拳擊手力量不相上下。

track 190

例 2, 4, 6, 8 are even numbers.

二、四、六、八是雙數。

例 They evened up the account with the bank.

他們同銀行結清帳目。

aboard

adv.	在船(或飛機、車)上、上船(或飛機、車)
prep.	在船(或飛機、車)上、上船(或飛機、車)

例 句

例 All aboard!

請各位上船(飛機／車)！

例 He climbed aboard.

他上了船(飛機／車)。

例 They went aboard the ship.

他們上了船。

presently

adv.	不久、一會兒、現在、目前

同義	immediately *adv.* 立即
	instantly *adv.* 即刻、立即

例 句

例 I'll be back presently.

我一會兒就回來。

例 He is presently living in New York.

他目前住在紐約。

深入分析

1. **presently** 過一會兒就去做某事，中間有段間隔。

☞ I will do the dishes presently, but I want to finish this story first.

　我馬上去洗碟子，不過我想先看完這篇故事。

2. **instantly**「立即」、「即刻」，指某事恰巧在此刻發生，一分鐘也沒有耽擱。

☞ I recognized her instantly when I saw her.

　我一看見她就立即認出她來了。

late

| adj. | 遲的、深夜的、已故的 |
| adv. | 晚地、遲地、黃昏地 |

反義　**early** adj. adv. 早的、提早的

例　句

例 Hurry up, we're late.

　快一點，我們遲到了。

例 She gave her late husband's clothes to charity.

　她將已逝的丈夫的衣物捐給慈善團體。

例 Tom was late for school.

　湯姆上學遲到了。

例 We got home very late.

　我們很晚才到家。

track 191

early

adj. 早的、早熟的

adv. 提早地

反義 late *adv. adj.* 晚的、遲的

例 句

例 It's still early, isn't it?

還很早，不是嗎？

例 "I'd like to see David." "You're early."

「我要見大衛。」「你早到了。」

lately

adv. 最近、不久前

同義 recently *adv.* 最近

例 句

例 Have you been to the cinema lately?

最近你去看過電影嗎？

例 I haven't seen him lately.

最近我一直沒見到他。

例 Just lately I have been wondering where to look for a job.

近來我一直在想到哪裡去找工作。

深入分析

1. lately 指從說話前不久持續到現在的一段時間，有時指過去特定時間。

☞ He has not been looking well lately.

他最近臉色一直不好。

2. late 指說話前不久的一段時間，多用於過去式。

☞ We didn't hear from him as late as last week.

直到上星期，我們還未收到他的信。

later

adj. 更遲的、較近的

adv. 後來、過一會兒

| 同義 | after *adj.* 後來 |

| 反義 | earlier *adj.* 更早的 |

例 句

例 She said she would speak to me later.

她說稍後要和我談談。

例 Why don't you call back later on, when he's sure to be here?

等確定他在的時候，你要不要晚一點再打來？

例 I'll call on you again later.

以後我會再來看你的。

深入分析

1. later 指在時間上「較遲」。

☞ the later part of the 18th century

18 世紀末

2. latter 指在順序上「較後」。

track 192

☞ the latter part of the 18th century

18世紀的後半世紀

latter

adv. 後者的(一般與 the 連用)、後一半的後者
(與 the 連用)

反義 the former 前者

例 句

例 I have studied English and Japanese; the former language I speak very well, but the latter one only a little.

我學英語和日語,前者我可以講得很好,而後者只能講一點。

例 In the latter part of the lesson we read our notes.

課堂的後半段時間我們讀筆記。

例 Of the two choices, I prefer the latter.

有兩個選擇,我選擇後者。

thereby

adv. 因此、從而

例 句

例 The strike closed most of the mines, thereby reducing the coal production by one half.

罷工使大多數煤礦關閉從而使煤產量下降一半。

track 192

例 It rained, thereby the football match was postponed.

天下雨，所以足球比賽延期了。

what

adv. 在哪一方、到什麼程度
pron. 什麼、怎麼樣
adj. 什麼、多麼

例 句

例 What are you going to do tonight?

你今天晚上要做什麼？

例 What would you like to have?

你想吃什麼？

例 What a pity!

真是遺憾！

例 "I have to look for a new job." "What for?"

「我應該要再找一份新工作。」「為什麼？」

track 193

how

adv. 多少、如何、多麼地

例 句

例 How much does it cost?

這個值多少錢？

例 Do you know how it happened?

你知道是怎麼發生的嗎？

track 193

例 How nice to see you!

真高興見到你。

例 "I'm Jack." "How do you do, I'm Tracy."

「我是傑克」「你好，我是崔西。」

when

adv. 什麼時候、何時

conj. 當…的時候

pron. 何時

例 句

例 When do you want to come?

你想什麼時候來？

例 Turn left when you get to the park.

到公園的時候左轉。

例 Since when has she taught here?

她從什麼時候開始在這兒教書的？

where

adv. 在哪裡、在…地方

conj. 到…地方

pron. 何處

例 句

例 Where are you going?

你要去哪裡？

例 I'll meet Tracy where I first met you.

我將在第一次見你的地方與崔西會面。

track 193

例 Where does David come from?

　大衛是哪裡人？

例 I asked him where to put it.

　我有問他要放在哪裡。

• why

adv. 為什麼、理由、所以…的原因

例 句

例 Why are you turning here?

　為什麼你要在這裡轉彎？

例 Why did you say so?

　你為什麼要這麼說？

例 "Can you help me with it?" "Sure. Why not?"

　「可以幫我一下嗎？」「好啊！有何不可！」

 track 194

who

pron. 誰、什麼人、…的人

例 句

例 Who did this?

　這是誰做的？

例 Who wrote this letter to you?

　誰寫這封信給你？

例 The girl who spoke is my best friend.

講話的那個女孩是我最要好的朋友。

somewhere

adv. 在某處、到某處

例 句

例 At last he found somewhere to park the car.

他終於找到某一地方停車。

例 You'll find the passage somewhere in the book.

你可以在本書某一地方找到這段文章。

whenever

conj. 無論如何、隨時、每當

例 句

例 Come whenever you like.

你喜歡什麼時候來就什麼時候來。

例 Whenever we see him, we speak to him.

每當我們看見他，都要與他說話。

track 194

again

adv. 再一次、再、又(恢復原狀)

例 句

例 He's late again.

他又遲到了。

例 "My name is David." "Come again?"

「我的名字是大衛。」「你說什麼？」

例 Thanks again.

再次感謝你。

but

conj. 可是、但是、而、除…外
prep. 除…外
adv. 只、僅僅、不過
pron. 沒有…不

例 句

例 It's not cheap, but it is very good.

這不便宜，但是品質很好。

例 No one saw it but me.　　 track 195

除了我沒有人看到。

例 It took David but a few days to learn it.

只不過幾天時間大衛就學會了。

例 Not a man but felt it.

沒有人不感覺到它。

and

conj. 和、與、同、又、而且、所以

例 句

例 David and I often go shopping at the weekend.

大衛和我經常在週末時去逛街。

例 Three and two is five.

三加二等於五。

例 There are two hundred and thirty boys in the school.

這所學校有230名男生。

例 You must stop, and at once, this sort of behavior.

你必須停止這種行為,而且必須立即停止。

例 Go straight on and you'll see a school.

一直走下去你就可以看到一所學校。

常見縮寫

DIY	自己動手做	Do It Yourself
BBQ	烤肉	barbecue
PYO	自己採摘的	pick-your-own
WC	洗手間	Water Closet
MRT	大眾捷運系統	Mass Rapid Transit
RV	休旅車	Recreational Vehicle
ID	身份標識號碼	Identity
CEO	總裁	Chief Executive Officer
VIP	貴賓	Very Important Person
ABC	美藉華人	American born Chinese
DINK	頂客族	Double Income No Kids
OL	粉領族	Office Lady
ET	外星人	extra-terrestrial
DJ	音樂節目廣播員	Disc Jockey
VJ	廣播節目主持人	Video Jockey
MC	司儀	Master of Ceremonies
EMT	急救員	Emergency Medical Technologist
POW	戰俘	Prisoner of War
FA	空服員	Flight Attendant
FE	飛航工程師	Flight Engineer
FO	副機長	First Officer
SOB	狗娘養的人	Son of a Bitch
PK	單挑	Play Killing
WP	遇雨順延	Weather Permitting

track 196

XL	特大號	Extra Large
L	大號	Large size
M	中號	Medium size
S	小號	Small size
GSM	全球通訊行動系統 Global System for Mobile Communication	
GPS	全球定位系統	Global Positioning System
PHS	低功率行動電話系統 Personal Handyphone System	
ATM	自動提款機	Automated Teller Machine
IC card	智能卡	Intelligent Card
IT	收入所得稅	Income Tax
TM	商標	Trade Mark
UC	大寫字母	uppercase
AI	人工智慧	Artificial Intelligence
MIT	台灣製造	Made in Taiwan
ISO	國際標準組織 International Standards Organization	
SOHO	個人工作室	small office home office
HQ	總部	headquarters
PR	公關	Public Relations
PC	個人電腦	Personal Computer
XP	微軟的作業系統	Office XP
MB	百萬位元組	MegaByte
GB	十億位元組	GigaByte
OEM	原設備製造商 Original Equipment Manufacturer	

track 196

IT	資訊技術	Information Technology
MSN	即時訊息	
SMS	簡訊	Short Message Service
Bug	電腦中的小故障	
VGA	視頻圖形陣列	Video Graphics Array
MIS	管理資訊系統 Management Information System	
MIDI	樂器數位介面 Musical Instrument Digital Interface	
PNP	隨插即用	Plug and Play
IC	積體電路	Integrated Circuit
IQ	智力商數	Intelligence Quotient
EQ	情緒智商	Emotional Quotient
AQ	逆境指數	Adversity Quotient
DOA	於到達時死亡	dead on arrival
CPR	心肺復甦術 cardiopulmonary resuscitation	
IPL	脈衝光	Intense Pulsed Light
ICU	加護病房	Intensive Care Unit
AIDS	愛滋病 Acquired Immune Deficiency Syndrome	
DNA	脫氧核糖核酸	Deoxyribonucleic Acid
HIV	人體免疫缺損病毒 Human Immunodeficiency Virus	
SARS	嚴重急性呼吸道症候群 Severe Acute Respiratory Syndrome	
DHF	登革熱 Dengue Hemorrhagic Fever	

track 197

VD	性病	Venereal Disease
PMS	經前症候群	pre-menstrual syndrome
ER	急診室	Emergency Room
RBC	紅血球	Red Blood Cell
WBC	白血球	White Blood Cell
ECG	心電圖	Electrocardiogram
BO	體味、狐臭	Body Odor
SPF	防曬係數	Sun Protection Factor
TLC	細心看護	Tender Loving Care

DDT　殺蟲劑
dichloro-dipheny-trichloro-ethane

| UFO | 幽浮 | Unidentified Flying Object |
| ATC | 航空交通管制 | Air Traffic Control |

CAA　民航局
Civil Aeronautics Administration

RCC　救援指揮中心　Rescue Control Center

YMCA 基督教青年會
Young Men's Christian Association

YWCA 基督教女青年會
Young Women's Christian Association

GRE　美國研究生入學考試
Graduate Record Examination

GMAT 企管入學測驗
Graduate Management Admissions Test

TOEFL 托福考試
Test of English as a Foreign Language

GEPT　全民英檢
General English Proficiency Test

 無敵**英語單字王**

GP	美國蓋洛普民意測驗 Gallup Poll	
ESL	第二語言英語 English as a Second Language	
NG	不理想的	No Good
OA	辦公室自動化	Official Automation
TU	工會	trade union
SAYE	由薪資中扣除的儲蓄存款 save-as-you-earn	
RC	加強型混凝土結構 Reinforced Concrete	
RE	不動產	Real Estate
Q&A	問題與解答	Question and Answer
FAQ	常見問題 Frequently Asked Questions	
i.e.	換言之	id est(拉丁文)＝that is
e.g.	例如 exempli gratia(拉丁文)＝for example	
PS	備註	Postscript
POB	郵政信箱	Post Office Box
R.S.V.P.	敬請回覆 repondez s'il vous plait (法文)＝please reply	
PTO	請閱背面	Please Turn Over
SASE	回郵信封 self-addressed stamped envelope	
FYI	供你參考	For Your Information
SD	快遞	Special Delivery
TWOV	過境無簽證	Transit Without Visa

track 198

ADSL	非同步數位用戶線路	
	Asymmetric Digital Subscriber Line	
COD	貨到付款	Cash On Delivery
CBD	預付款	Cash Before Delivery
GNP	國民生產總值	Gross National Product
QC	品質管控	Quality Control
B&B	只提供早餐和床鋪的住宿	
	Bed and Breakfast	
DUI	酒醉駕車	driving under the influence
ESP	搖頭性愛派對	Ecstasy Sex Party
VR	虛擬實境	Virtual Reality
FM	一種廣播調頻	Frequency Modulation
AM	一種廣播調頻	Amplitude Modulation
WAP	無線軟體應用通訊協定	
	Wireless Application Protocol	
GPRS	封包無線通訊服務	
	General Packet Radio System	
TAM	電視收視率	
	Television Audience Measurement	
OB	戶外轉播	Outside Broadcast
MVP	最佳運動員	Most Valuable Player
MTV	音樂電視	Music TV
ICRT	國際社區電台	
	International Community Radio Taipei	
HBO	一家專門提供電影節目的有線電視公司	
	Home Box Office	

MTV	音樂電視	Music TV
R&B	節奏藍調	Rhythm and Blues
R&R	搖滾	Rock & Roll
DVD	數位視訊影碟	Digital Video Disk
CCTV	閉路電視	closed circuit television
LCD	液晶顯示	Liquid Crystal Display
LD	雷射影碟	Laser Disk
MD	迷你光碟	Mini Disk
CD	光碟	compact disk
AV	視聽的	audio-visual
AV	成人影片	Adult Video
BC	西元前	before Christ
AD	西元 anno Domini (拉丁文)=in the year of our Lord	
GMT	格林威治標準時間 Greenwich Mean Time	
PST	太平洋標準時間	Pacific Standard Time
PDT	太平洋夏令時間	Pacific Daylight Time
ASAP	盡快	As Soon As Possible
DOB	出生日期	Date of Birth
YOB	出生年份	Year of Birth
a.m.	午前	ante meridiem
p.m.	下午	post meridiem
UV	紫外線的	ultraviolet

WORLD

THE BEST ENGLISH CONVERSATION FOR VACATIONS

想出國自助旅遊嗎？

不論是出境、入境、住宿，
或是觀光、交通、解決三餐，

**通通可以自己一手包辦的
「旅遊萬用手冊」**

永續圖書
線上購物網

www.foreverbooks.com.tw

◆ 加入會員即享活動及會員折扣。

◆ 每月均有優惠活動，期期不同。

◆ 新加入會員三天內訂購書籍不限本數金額，
即贈送精選書籍一本。（依網站標示為主）

專業圖書發行、書局經銷、圖書出版

永續圖書總代理：

五觀藝術出版社、培育文化、棋茵出版社、大拓文化、讚
品文化、雅典文化、大億文化、璞申文化、智學堂文化、
語言鳥文化

活動期內，永續圖書將保留變更或終止該活動之權利及最終決定權。